The Doomed Doctor

Doro Banyon Cozy Historical Mysteries-Book 6

D.S. Lang

Ebook ISBN: 978-1-962029-15-4

Paperback ISBN: 978-1-962039-16-1

Cover designer-Karen Phillips

Editor-Alyssa Colton

In loving memory of my sweet Izzy, the inspiration for Tee, and a doggie detective in her own right.
See you, and the rest of the family (people and pets) over the Rainbow Bridge.

Prologue

Mid-April 1930

Shortly after midnight on Sunday

As Dorothea Banyon, Everett Mallow, and their little dog Tee ambled through the Michaw College campus, she took a deep breath of cool air and blew it out. At the same time, Doro clasped Ev's arm more tightly. Walking beside him in the quiet of late night with only the moon and post lights to dispel darkness usually soothed her spirit. But not tonight.

"That's a big sigh," Ev murmured as he patted her hand. "Releasing pent-up stress?"

"Trying to, I suppose." But tension remained. Would the final event of Founder's Day weekend, this afternoon's brunch, be spoiled? That seemed all too likely.

"How about a walk in the park? We could head over to where the pool is going in. It's supposed to open on Memorial Day, so progress should be noticeable by now."

The suggestion, Doro felt sure, was meant to distract her, and any distraction was welcome. "I'd like to see it. I haven't had time to look for the past couple of weeks."

The pair, along with Tee who led the way, continued to the far end of the park. Doro relished the feel of her soft hand in Ev's callused one, and seeing their small canine at the end of the lead in her free hand brought a smile to her lips. Dogs delighted in the present moment. People should, too, so Doro tried not to think about the crime casting a dark spell over the college's big celebration. Perhaps, they would solve it before brunch. But how?

When they reached the place where new post lights had been erected, but were not all on, Ev spoke again. "We need to watch where we're going, since it's dimmer over this way. With the construction, there could be ruts. Even though we changed out of our party duds, we don't want to walk through mud, and there could be some after last week's rain."

Doro chuckled. Her dancing shoes were in her closet, but her current footwear, sturdy Oxfords, was not perfect for traversing rough ground. Boots would be better. She clasped his hand tighter. "I'll lean on you."

"Good." The single word echoed with emotion, but he said nothing more.

As they went on, Doro noted the lamps near the pool area provided some illumination, enough to see concrete had been poured as decking. "It's a nice size."

"It is," Ev agreed. Before he could say more, Tee yanked hard on the leash. Doro tried to hold her back, but the little dog pulled free and darted toward the pool. "Oh, no. She's so curious. What if she falls in and hits the concrete bottom?" Tee could be seriously injured, or worse. The idea made Doro sick at heart.

Ev whistled, but Tee kept running. Both he and Doro called out to no avail. The pup kept racing toward the unfinished pool.

"I'll get her." With that, he dashed off.

"She never acts so wild," Doro called as she followed him.

"No, she doesn't, but she's intent on whatever is laying on the downslope. I can't see exactly what it is. Maybe some trash. Or an animal. I hope it isn't an injured raccoon, because Tee would come out on the bad end of any battle with one. I'll have to climb down. Otherwise, I can't get close enough to grab her leash."

Ev shed his shoes and rolled up his pant legs. Meanwhile, he kept talking to the little dog, who continued to yip and jump around. Although Tee was always energetic, her behavior was unusual. Why was she so agitated? With her pulse pounding in her ears, Doro stared into the semi-darkness. When Ev reached the pup, he petted her and then, froze.

Doro watched with growing trepidation. Even in the dimness, she saw him move further into the pool and bend down. The dog disappeared, only to resurface dragging a man's shoe along. A very distinctive shoe. A two-toned brown spectator wing-tip. A gasp escaped Doro. Over the last few days, Doro had only seen two people with that type of footwear. Those men, whom she had known as a coed, had been two of the Michaw College alumni attending Founder's Weekend. Only an hour or so ago, she had seen them both at the dance. "Is he all right?"

After turning to look over his shoulder at Doro, Ev shook his head. "No. He's dead."

Chapter One

Thursday afternoon

Two cups of coffee failed to lift the weight of fatigue from Doro. Despite the fog lingering in her head, her mind churned with a long list of duties yet to complete before she left the library. A glance at her wristwatch showed the time to be three-thirty. She needed to press hard to finish everything, but she would because leaving late was not an option, not when she and Ev were going to dinner and a movie in nearby Sylvania. Anticipation spread through Doro as she imagined an entire evening with her sweetheart. She couldn't repress a grin. Sweetheart. He was sweet, and he was definitely in her heart.

"You look mighty happy for someone sitting behind a desk stacked with papers."

Doro looked up to see her best friend, Agatha Darwine, standing in the door of her office. "Come in and sit down."

After removing a stack of books from a chair facing Doro's desk, Aggie took a seat. "So, are you happy for any particular reason?" Amusement shone in her hazel eyes.

"I am," Doro replied with complete candor. "Ev and I are going out tonight. Just the two of us. We haven't spent much time together for the last couple of weeks."

"Because you've been occupied as chairwoman of the Founder's Day celebration."

A sigh escaped Doro as she leaned forward to brace her elbows on the desk. "You've been working hard, too."

"But not as hard as you," Aggie observed. "Everyone comes to the chairwoman with questions—large or small—and you handle them all."

"I can't deny fielding various concerns, but others have pitched in," Doro agreed. "Now, almost every detail is in place, and we're ready to welcome alumni and former professors starting tomorrow morning."

The jangling of the telephone on Doro's desk interrupted. "I'm regretting that a phone was put in here," she murmured before picking it up. Just hearing the name of the caller, after the operator made the connection, had Doro gripping the earpiece and candlestick base tighter. Listening to the woman's long diatribe had her stomach knotting. Whenever her caller took a breath, Doro squeezed in a "Yes, ma'am." Or a "No, ma'am." Whichever fit the gap. When the conversation came to an end, the telephone nearly slid out of her sweaty palm.

"Who was that?" Aggie asked.

"Mrs. Smith."

"The woman who's donating the valuable book?"

"Yes. She just spoke with President Adams, but I need to know her wishes, too. Or so she said. A decision has been made, by her, about placing the manuscript in the glass cabinet in the entrance of College Hall for two days. I knew it was under consideration, along with precautions to keep it safe, but I hoped she'd change her mind. She hasn't. And she won't. In addition, she made it crystal clear that, if I want her support when my boss retires, I won't lodge further objections."

Aggie's eyes went wide. "She threatened to stop you from becoming library director."

"Exactly," Doro released a pent-up breath. "Mrs. Smith wants the priceless treasure, her words, to be seen by as many people as possible, and she expects the college to provide security while it's on display. I knew she told President Adams that yesterday, which is when I objected. Anyhow, there was a break-in at her home last month. The book was in their safe, but the first floor was ransacked. She's sure it will be fine here."

Aggie nodded. "I recall hearing about it. Until the formal gift giving, you'd think Mrs. Smith would want the book kept in President Adams' safe instead of in a glass showcase in a very public place."

"Both Mr. and Mrs. Smith want it displayed, according to her," Doro replied. "Maybe they don't figure they'll get enough credit for donating such a valuable item if it's not on display during the entire weekend."

Aggie pursed her lips. "The Smiths want plenty of credit for their generosity."

A smile tugged at Doro's mouth. "They're giving a priceless book to the college, and they want everyone to know. President

Adams will try to change their minds, I think, but I won't voice my opinion again. If it's in the showcase, and that's quite likely, guarding it will fall on Wade and Ev. They already discussed it with our president." Wade Lammers was not only the town constable, he was Aggie's fiancé.

All amusement left Aggie's expression. "Then, they won't have free time this weekend, but neither will we."

"President Adams still has an opportunity to dissuade her. When I spoke with him earlier, he planned to point out that the book will be in the locked case behind the library's circulation desk after the presentation, so people can see it there. Just not in such a close-up, high-traffic, unmonitored spot as College Hall."

Aggie nodded. "To my way of thinking, it's a safer location, since the desk here is always manned when the library is open. After hours, the building is more secure than ever with the new locks on all doors."

Doro nodded. "President Adams insisted on that. The book is rare and valuable, and he doesn't want anything happening to it." Worry clutched at her insides. Neither did she. "It's a generous gift. As of yesterday, the plan was for Ev and Wade to take turns standing guard. Ev told me last evening that they were preparing, but you must know that."

"Wade mentioned it in passing, but he didn't give details. We barely had a private moment because his children were filled with school news when I stopped by the office. We haven't talked since then." Her lips pursed. "The Smiths donate a lot of money to the college, which puts our president in a pickle."

"It sure does," Doro agreed. Now, she was in an equally ten-uous predicament. Further objections would put her lifelong goal of being library director completely out of reach.

A sympathetic expression blanketed Aggie's face. "It seems like an odd donation," Aggie murmured. "As an English pro-fessor, I appreciate its value, but I would've given it to a major museum."

"I see the logic in having it here. The author was a graduate of Michaw College, and he went on to teach here before becoming a full-time writer. This book is a first edition of his first book, which was highly acclaimed. Only two other copies still exist." The anxiety plaguing Doro surfaced in her tone and in her next words. "Other valuable books have been stolen and sold in New York City. While Michaw isn't a big town, the thefts along Book Row were well publicized in many quarters."

"I'd love to visit there some day. Blocks of book shops appeal to me," Aggie murmured.

"Me, too," Doro said. "And it's the center of the antiquities market, so the theft ring working there made sense."

"True, but who in Michaw would be involved in that?"

"Word has spread that the book will be here. I know theft seems unlikely, but it is valuable. Priceless almost." Although the possibility of the manuscript being stolen seemed all too real, Doro forced a smile. "Once it's in the library, I'll rest easier, although probably not until the term ends."

"We can all rest then," Aggie agreed.

After another scan of her cluttered desk, Doro looked back at her friend. She drummed her fingers on her desk as she consid-ered how to relay some news—probably unwelcome news. "A couple more RSVPs arrived in this morning's mail. They were waiting for me after the committee meeting, so I haven't had a chance to tell you."

A puzzled expression covered Aggie's face. "I'm only in charge of decorations. Since the dinner tomorrow evening and the dance on Saturday night will both be in the auditorium, we'll only need to move tables in-between and freshen bouquets. The Sunday afternoon brunch will mean decorating the main dining hall on campus, but a few more people won't alter plans for any of those events. The town bakery will provide sweets for the refreshment table at the dance. If there are a lot more people, we can increase the order, but a couple of extras won't matter."

Doro pressed her palms together and put her hands to her chin. "It's not the number of extra people, and I'm sure who's coming won't make a difference after all this time." She smiled. "You're happily engaged to Wade, and you'll be married soon." Although her friend and the town constable had not set a date, the pair had become betrothed at the town and college's annual Sweetheart Ball on Valentine's Day.

"In the near future, we will," Aggie agreed, "but what does that have to do with more RSVPs?"

Doro took a deep breath and folded her hands on the desk. "One was from Rudyard Ingram, which I'm sure doesn't matter to you. I mean, you and Wade are deeply in love, so an old beau is of no importance. None at all." Realizing she was blathering, Doro stopped. When her friend made no reply, Doro studied Aggie's face, which had lost its fair color. Did she still have some feelings for Rudyard? "Aggie, are you all right?"

Several seconds of silence preceded Aggie's response. "Of course. I'm just surprised. Rud has never been to any campus events since he graduated. I wonder why he's coming this year."

"Hard to say, but he scribbled a note on his card saying he's looking forward to renewing old friendships."

Aggie gripped the chair arms until her knuckles showed white. "Interesting."

"That's a ubiquitous word."

"It fits the situation. Rud was involved in many campus activities as a student, so I've always found it odd that he's never returned. Maybe he kept in touch with others by mail."

Although Aggie had not mentioned Rud in years, Doro wondered if her friend was really so unaffected. She had not been a decade ago. Back then, and for months after Rudyard's graduation, Aggie had been upset, almost bereft, at his lack of communication. "You haven't brought him up in a long time, but I thought you should know he's coming."

"I'm glad you told me, although it makes no difference." Aggie moved her hands to her lap, where she clasped and unclasped them.

"Seeing Rud won't bother you?"

"Why should it?"

Aggie's terse tone, so unlike her, caught Doro off-guard. "It shouldn't. I just wondered." Doro let her voice trail off. Something was amiss, but what?

Aggie's knuckles went white. "It isn't what you're probably thinking. I have no feelings for Rud any longer and haven't had for years. It's more being embarrassed that I ever did. No one likes being reminded of foolishness."

While the statements did not reveal the heart of the problem, they offered reassurances that Aggie was over Rudyard Ingram. "Why be embarrassed? The two of you got close after he worked with us to clear your name and save your scholarship." As always, when she thought about first meeting Aggie, Doro smiled. "It was terrible when Professor Folsing accused you of negligence after his test went missing, but something wonderful came out of it. You and I met."

An answering grin lightened Aggie's countenance. "I was terrified when Folsing ranted and raved about me not doing my job as a student worker properly. The professor was set on getting my scholarship revoked. If he had, I wouldn't be here now, because I couldn't have afforded to stay in school. I'm not sure I would've fought back without your assistance, and your dad's, too."

"Dad being a professor in the same department as Folsing was a good thing."

"It was," Aggie agreed with another smile. "Your father hiring me as his student worker for the rest of my undergraduate studies was also great. So was rooming with you."

Although Doro was a year younger than Aggie, the two had shared quarters for three years. During that time, they had grown as close as sisters. And they still were, which was why Doro was puzzled by Aggie's mention of embarrassment. "Rud played a role, too, and you two spent time together."

"I'm grateful for his help, so it will be nice to see him again." The lack of emotion in her voice failed to support the assertion.

Her friend's reaction confused Doro. "You seemed smitten with him. And he with you. You never said exactly what happened, but you were upset."

"I imagined there was more to our friendship than was real." A genuine smile chased the shadows from Aggie's face. "It was a long time ago. What I felt for Rud was a girlish crush. Besides, we were from completely different families and circumstances. It was never meant to be. And I love Wade. I can't wait to share the rest of my life with him and his family and create a bigger family."

A pleasant possibility popped into Doro's mind. "Maybe you'll announce a wedding date this weekend."

Aggie chuckled. "You'd like me to spite Rud?"

"Of course not." When her friend's eyebrows shot up, Doro shrugged. "At least he'll see you have a good man now."

"I have a wonderful man, and so do you."

Tenderness spread through Doro. "We're lucky." A tap at the door interrupted, and she glanced up to see Ev. When he swept his cap off, his clipped brown hair became visible. With one hand, he brushed an errant lock off his handsome face. Doro's heart fluttered. Clad in his charcoal gray campus security officer uniform, he was every inch the lawman he had been all his adult life.

"The two of you are lucky?" he asked. "In some new way?"

Although she and Ev had shared their feelings for one another, Doro hesitated to blurt out a reply. Her friend had no such qualms.

"We're lucky to have good men in our lives," Aggie told him.

Ev's silver gaze, glittering with satisfaction, moved to Doro. "Wade and I are the lucky ones."

His sincerity was echoed by Doro. "All four of us are fortunate."

"Undeniably true," Aggie added.

"What brought the idea up?" Ev asked as he looked from one young woman to the other.

Uneasiness replaced pleasure inside Doro. Had Aggie ever mentioned Rud to Wade? Since she did not know, Doro made a banal remark. "Just chatting about various couples."

"We were," Aggie agreed before jumping to her feet. "I'll give you two some privacy. See you tomorrow morning at the welcome desk, Doro. You and I have the first shift."

Doro nodded. "See you then."

After Aggie left, Ev folded his tall, lean frame into the seat vacated by her. "What other couples were you discussing?"

The query was natural enough, but Doro hesitated to answer. Even if Aggie had discussed Rud with Wade, would she want her prior connection to him being broadcast? The question swirled through Doro's mind. Before a solution arose, Ev spoke again.

"Is there something you don't want to tell me? Some confidence between best friends?"

For a moment, Doro searched his face. Was he upset, hurt, curious? She was uncertain. "Do you and Wade keep secrets between you?"

A grin kicked up the corners of his mouth. "Didn't someone once say answering a question with a question is an equivocation?"

Doro laughed. "I'm the one who has said that, and more than once."

As he lifted his chin, the light of amusement glittered like quicksilver in his gaze. "That's right. It was you."

His reaction lifted Doro's spirits. "So, do the two of you discuss things privately?"

Ev's shoulders went up and down. "In regard to what we're talking about right now, Wade and I seldom comment on various couples. However, we've both shared how fortunate we are to be courting such extraordinary women." As he spoke, Ev leaned forward, reached for her hand and brought it to his lips. After a quick kiss in the palm, he released his hold and sat back. "Not proper in the library, I know."

Her hand tingled from the featherlight caress. "Perhaps not, but we'll be together later." By current standards, the comment might be considered brazen, but Doro—while not a flapper—was a thoroughly modern young woman. Although Ev was her first beau, she did not feel shy with him. Not any longer.

He grinned again. "After such a busy week, I'll be glad for us to have some time to ourselves."

"It's been hectic," she agreed.

His gaze went to her cluttered desk. "It looks like you have more work to do before leaving."

She put a hand to her forehead. "Unfortunately, I got behind with library duties due to being chairwoman for this weekend's events. We had our last meeting this morning, so everyone is set for the arrival of guests tomorrow."

"From what I just heard, you and Aggie are still greeting the first wave?"

"We are." Anxiety filtered through Doro as she considered who would come while she and Aggie were on duty. Rud's note indicated he would be among the early arrivals. Was Aggie really as unaffected as she claimed? Doro hoped so.

Ev's gaze narrowed on her. "You don't seem enthusiastic about it. I thought you'd be happy to see old schoolmates and former professors. Your family has a long history with the college."

What he said was accurate. Her great-grandfather, grandfather and father had all attended Michaw College and, for years, her dad had been a professor. Only her mother contracting consumption, and needing a different climate had taken her father away. Since Doro's uncle had lived in Colorado at the time, her mother went to a sanitarium near her brother's home. When her health improved, she had stayed on, due to physicians' advice. At that point, Dr. Ebediah John Banyon had taken a teaching position at Colorado College while Doro had opted to stay in Michaw. Her choice was partly because her Gramma Rose lived nearby, and also because the town was home in a way Colorado Springs could never be, despite her parents living there.

"We go back several generations, and it'll be lovely to see familiar faces again."

"Are you disappointed because your parents aren't coming?"

Although that was not the reason for her current state of mind, Doro wished her mother and father were present. "I understand why they aren't. Mother's health is much better in the Springs, and coming home might trigger another downturn. None of us want that. This time of year can be chilly and damp here, which would be bad for her."

"But you'd like to see them."

"I would."

For several moments, Ev watched her as if looking for some telltale sign. "You haven't mentioned visiting them this summer."

The comment surprised Doro, mostly because she had not given the idea much consideration. "No. I haven't thought about it."

Tension laced his lean body as his gaze searched her face. "You've been going every summer since your mother left Michaw, right?"

Why was Ev asking when he knew the answer? "I have, but things are different now. You and I are courting." When his shoulders slumped, Doro realized he had been rigid with doubt. "You didn't think I'd be away for three months, did you?"

A long sigh escaped him. "You went away on a couple of days' notice last summer."

Regret traced her spine. "At the time, we weren't courting. We weren't even stepping out."

A bleak expression blanketed his features. "Because you didn't want to," Ev pointed out in a grim tone.

"No, not because I didn't want to," she reminded him. "Back then, I still put being library director ahead of everything else. It'd been my dream as far back as I could remember. Since the college didn't employ married women, I resolved to stay a spinster. At least I did until last summer. We've discussed that." After a glance at the door, Doro laid her hand on his arm. "In August, when I was kidnapped by the killer on our train, I didn't spend time thinking about my job or about being promoted. I thought about you and how much I wished we'd parted on better terms." While Doro had told him as much in the past, she wanted to dispel any lingering doubt on his part. Although their courtship might not progress to engagement and marriage, Doro didn't want misunderstandings to linger.

He smiled. "I'm glad about that, but I'm just as glad the college changed its policy last term. Now, you can be a wife and the library director."

"I'm beyond lucky to have a man who doesn't think women belong at home."

Ev winked. "You belong wherever you want to be, but none of this explains why you seem troubled. And Aggie did, too. Wade acts as happy as ever, so I wouldn't think there were problems between the two of them."

"Not at all." Doro squeezed his hand. "Aggie is uneasy about someone who's coming this weekend, although she claims it's fine."

Ev's forehead creased. "The professor who threatened her scholarship? I thought he passed away."

"He did," Doro replied. After hesitating for a heartbeat, she went on. "There's a fellow from our undergraduate days who is attending. This is the first time he's been back since his graduation."

A perplexed expression covered Ev's face. "Was he mean to Aggie? I know she can be sensitive, and I assume she was even more so as a girl."

The observations were more evidence that Ev was astute. "Rud wasn't precisely mean. In fact, he helped us solve the mystery of the lost exam, which we've mentioned to you and Wade. Back then, he was sweet on Aggie."

Ev sat up straighter. "Was she sweet on him?"

His direct question made Doro shift restlessly in her chair. She released his hand and returned to the seat behind her desk. Gathering her thoughts was easier when she was not so close to him. Before she formed a response, Ev braced his elbows on his knees and put his head in his hands.

"She was and still is," he murmured.

"No, not at all," Doro rushed to say. When Ev caught her gaze, she continued. "They studied together, went to some football games, took in movies in Sylvania."

"They stepped out often."

"Off-and-on," Doro murmured. "Now, she says it wasn't serious, but she was upset when Rud didn't stay in touch. Just now, she mentioned not being from the same background. Whether Rud ever said as much is a question mark. I should've asked what she meant, but the conversation moved on."

"I suppose a first love is hard to forget." Dismay clouded Ev's gaze. "Does Wade know about Ingram? He never mentioned the name to me."

Doro drummed her fingers on the desk. "Aggie didn't say. My guess is she hasn't told him, because he might be upset."

"Wade is a widower, so I doubt he'd be bothered that Aggie was smitten with a college boy years ago. If she still cares for the guy, that's a different story." He narrowed his gaze. "You're sure she doesn't?"

"She doesn't, and she says what she felt for Rud was only a crush, not real love. Thinking back, she was lonely and alone.

Her dad died shortly before she started college, her mother had been gone for a few years, and her brother stayed in France after the war. Rud gave Aggie a sense of security, I think."

Ev clasped his hands in front of him. "That makes sense, but you're certain she isn't carrying a torch for the guy?"

"Absolutely sure. She loves Wade."

His features relaxed. "Good, because he loves her."

Despite the reassurance, anxiety assailed Doro. "You won't tell him about Rud."

"Certainly not, but Aggie should—if she hasn't already."

Since she agreed, Doro nodded. "I'll speak with her when I get back to Wheaton Hall. I don't know if she ever mentioned Rud to Wade, but I'll find out." With reluctance, she moved to a different topic. "Now, as much as I'd like to chat more with you, I should finish my paperwork, so I can have tonight and the weekend free—except for Founder's Day events."

A smile lifted one corner of his mouth. "Considering the fact that you're the chairwoman of the whole shebang, you'll be busy. Unfortunately, so will I."

His assertion reminded Doro of the rare manuscript. "President Adams will try to convince the donors not to have the book put in the entrance of College Hall. If he does, you and Wade won't have to stand guard duty at night on top of your regular work."

His lips flattened. "From what I know, that's unlikely. The Smiths are set on as many people as possible seeing her donation."

Simmering anxiety bubbled to the surface. "I know. She called me a few minutes ago to say I need to end my objections." Doro did not mention the woman's threat.

Ev's gaze narrowed. "Will you?"

With reluctance, she nodded. "Saying more won't help at this point. President Adams will make another attempt, but he isn't apt to succeed."

"I agree. Doing what big donors want is important, especially in tough times. Evidently, the October stock market crash didn't affect the Smiths, but plenty of others lost a lot of money."

The observation reignited Doro's concern. "What about the book being taken? We didn't have a chance to discuss that yesterday."

He rubbed the back of his neck. "With fraternity prankster week about to start, that's a concern. Of course, if pledges take it, the book should come back in short order."

Something in his tone disturbed her. "Do you think someone else would steal it? It's very valuable." She shared some of her conversation with Aggie.

"The truth is, we can't completely discount a theft. News of the donation was in the alumni bulletin, the local newspaper, and in the Toledo papers. Mrs. Smith made sure of the last, since she lives in the area." His nostrils flared with a sharp intake of breath. "Crime is always a problem, but more folks are struggling now. Wade and I are both concerned that desperation may lead someone to go for the book. Word has been out about it long enough that a dishonest person could've already checked out how and where to sell it."

"There is a market for rare books." Doro repeated what she had shared with Aggie about thefts from bookstores in New York City.

"I heard a little about that. One of my colleagues at the Prohibition Bureau was a copper in New York when some of the thefts along Book Row occurred."

"Did he work on the cases?"

Ev shook his head. "No, but he heard a lot about them. In some instances, bookstore employees colluded with the thieves and got a cut of the profit."

"I didn't know that," Doro murmured. "I can't imagine that anyone here would work with thieves. Besides, even though there's been publicity about the book donation, how many local people would attempt that type of theft? They need a market for it. I can't think of one alumnus or community member who would have that knowledge, and I hope none would be so dishonest."

"How much do you know about all the alumni visiting for the weekend?"

The question increased her anxiety. "Some stay in touch with the college, but a fair number don't."

"A few must live in big cities where they could access the black market for rare books. The ring in New York was very active, and it targeted libraries, as well as bookshops."

"I hadn't heard that," Doro murmured. "I can see how that could occur, since most libraries don't have strong security. President Adams made sure ours is much better,"

"Due to the valuable book being donated," Ev replied.

"Right." Doro reconsidered plans for the weekend. "At least, the Smiths won't arrive until tomorrow. President Adams won't put the book in the case until during dinner, and I know he's arranged for two of the custodians to guard it then, so you and Wade can attend."

"It'll be fine. We'll take over after escorting you girls home." His gaze strayed to her mouth. "We won't be able to linger for a few private moments."

Her lips joined her palm in tingling. "But we have tonight to ourselves."

His silver gaze sparkled. "Yes, we do. See you at six o'clock."

After Doro watched Ev stride out of her office and into the library, she returned to work. Getting it out of the way would free up Sunday evening, since the last event was the brunch after church services. Most visitors would leave by late afternoon. If the weather continued to be fine, she and Ev could take a picnic supper to their favorite escape outside town. Anticipation made her dig into work with gusto.

Chapter Two

The rest of Thursday afternoon passed in a blur of work. When Doro returned to Wheaton Hall, she had only fifteen minutes to talk with Aggie, who revealed she had shared information about Rudyard Ingram with Wade. Satisfied with the knowledge that Wade would not be blindsided, Doro pushed all worries to a far corner of her mind and enjoyed her evening with Ev.

Because they went to a late movie, the pair did not get back to Michaw until midnight. Taking Tee, who had waited patiently in Doro's apartment, out was a must. Since Doro and Ev shared custody of the little fluffy black dog, found almost two years earlier as a stray puppy, both walked her around campus. The weeknight curfew for students, eleven o'clock, had passed, so Doro and Ev enjoyed the peace and solitude. While he held Tee's lead, Doro tucked one hand into the crook of his arm. Spending time with him and watching the small canine was a source of joy and comfort. Tee delighted in sniffing along the winding paths and being showered with attention from her two people. To Doro's way of thinking, ending the day with her sweetheart and their pup was perfect. All concerns fell away as she savored the time together. Few words passed between Doro and Ev, but she felt the connection. Was it unbreakable? She gripped his arm a little tighter and hoped it would be forever.

Ev glanced down at Doro. "Are you all right?"

"Sure. I was just thinking."

"You've got so much going on that I'm not surprised. Anything I can help with?"

The question reminded Doro of her concern about the manuscript. "You're already helping by escorting the manuscript to the library after the ceremony on Sunday, and by taking guard duty for two nights."

"It's part of both my jobs—campus security officer and deputy constable. And part of Wade's job, too. After Sunday, the book should be safe in the library cabinet. Until then, I understand your worry. Any valuable item can lure thieves."

"I'd like to think alumni and retired faculty wouldn't consider stealing, but the alumni magazine could be passed to anyone. The same with city newspapers."

A pensive expression lined his face. "You and Aggie would recognize strangers better than Wade and I, so let us know if you see someone who isn't attached to the college."

Doro chewed on her lower lip as she considered his comment. "Many alumni will bring spouses, and we won't know them on sight. We should be introduced, though."

"All right. We'll watch for anyone not associated with the event, not that crooks will surface long before a robbery." When

Tee stopped again to sniff, Ev turned toward Doro. "It's unlikely that anyone will try to steal the manuscript, but being cautious is wise."

Several moments of silence passed while Doro considered the assertion. Although she was sure Ev sought to pacify her, Doro nodded. "I agree." She knew she did not sound convinced when he replied.

"Don't worry. Nothing will happen to that manuscript, if we can help it."

"I know you'll do your best. I don't usually fret so much."

"You're worn out. Let's get you back to Wheaton Hall, so you can rest. I'll keep Tee overnight, so you won't have to get her out in the morning before going to the welcome table. She can make my morning rounds with me."

"Sounds like a fine idea for her." Doro bent down to pet the small dog who wagged her long, plume-like tail wildly. "I'll miss you tonight, but I'll see you tomorrow, little girl."

Tee yipped in response and, as she and Ev headed away, the dog looked back and twitched her tail once more. Doro waved before going to her apartment and climbing into bed. Despite her concerns, she was asleep within moments.

‸

Friday morning came far too early for Doro, who—despite deep fatigue—had not stayed asleep. Instead, she had woken at four o'clock and laid wide awake. Her mind had churned with various tasks and with protecting the manuscript. Although Ev and Wade would handle that, her concern was amplified by knowing

Rud Ingram would arrive soon. As she dressed and ate, Doro mulled over the day ahead. She was not looking forward to seeing Rud again, but she would put up a friendly front—for Aggie's sake. Would Rud treat her well? He better, or he'd answer to Doro. And probably to Wade, too. After washing and dressing, Doro went on her way.

When she got to her friend's apartment, Aggie was still debating what to wear. A pile of discards laid on her bed while several other outfits hung from the hall tree in the corner of her bedroom. Doro looked around in shock. "You don't fret over what to wear anymore, unless it's a special occasion, and you want to look particularly pretty for Wade."

Aggie's expression remained solemn. "Wade compliments me even when I wear something less than flattering. Last week, I was in his mother's kitchen helping her make pies. I had a threadbare apron on, and I was covered in flour. He came in and said I looked wonderful, which I didn't."

Doro pursed her lips. "He loves you, so you're always beautiful to him. Doesn't he always seem handsome to you?"

A half-shrug lifted one of Aggie's shoulders. "Of course."

"Then, accept the compliments." Doro glanced at her watch. "As for today, you should choose your clothes soon, because we need to be at the welcome table in thirty minutes."

With a sigh, Aggie went to the hall tree and pulled a navy skirt and matching top off. She held it up to herself. "What about this one? It's not colorful, but it fits well, and your grandmother said it looks good on me."

Since Doro's Gramma Rose MacLaren, who remained abreast of styles even in her seventies, often went shopping with the two friends, Aggie listened to the older woman's advice. As did Doro. "It does, but all of your clothes are stylish and flattering. I don't understand why you're debating your attire. It's not like you. Not any more" As she spoke, Doro felt realization hit her. "You want to make Rudyard sorry he didn't stay in touch."

Aggie clutched the outfit closer to her. "It's not that exactly. It's more how I was back when I was a student. Dowdy, meek, and foolish. I no longer care for him, but I want to be seen as successful and satisfied."

Doro went to the hall tree, where a bright skirt and top still hung. "The shades of green in this one give a hint of spring. Why don't you wear it with those cute shoes we bought on our last shopping trip in Toledo? Didn't you say this ensemble is one of Wade's favorites?"

Aggie nodded. "It is."

"Then, it will do double-duty by pleasing him and making Rud feel foolish."

"A twinge of regret from Rud is all I hope to achieve. It's far more important to please Wade as much as he pleases me." She put the navy ensemble back and picked up the green one. "I feel silly for wanting even that much of a reaction. It's been over a decade since Rud's graduation. I shouldn't care what he thinks of me now, and yesterday is the first time he's come to my mind in years." Dismay clouded her eyes. "Maybe I'm not as confident as I figured."

Doro crossed the room to lay a hand on Aggie's arm. "You're an accomplished professor and a talented poet. You're recognized for your achievements in both areas, and as an important part of Michaw College. You're liked and respected by students, colleagues and townspeople. Although you're still a little shy, you haven't lacked poise for years and years."

Delicate color crept into Aggie's freckled cheeks. "I appreciate the support, but that's mostly in my professional life. Social situations still unnerve me."

"Concentrate on how you feel with those important to you. People like you as a person. Wade, his children, his mother and his sister adore you. I love you like a sister, and my family loves you, too. So does Ev." When Aggie still looked hesitant, Doro continued. "It's natural to want to show people from our pasts that they didn't give us enough credit. That doesn't make us weak or needy."

For a moment, Aggie studied Doro's face. "You've felt like you had something to prove at times."

Doro nodded. "You know I have. Last year, I didn't want to make a basket for the May Days picnic auction because I had a terrible experience as a girl. Only my fathers' friends bid on my picnic baskets after that awful boy in my class insisted that I poisoned him. Then, I quit submitting one. I wasn't a good cook, but my food wasn't dangerous."

Aggie put a hand to her mouth but some sound escaped.

"Are you laughing?" Doro's lips twitched despite her best effort to look stern.

Her friend shook her head. "Not at all. Besides, Ev outbid everyone on your basket last May Day."

"The competition wasn't steep, but he went way above what I expected," Doro murmured, as warmth filled her at the memory. While they had been at odds about courting, she and Ev had enjoyed sharing her basket. "It felt good to see my old schoolmates gawk in surprise that a young man—and a handsome one—purchased my meal. Just like it was lovely to step on the floor with him for the special dance at the Sweetheart Ball in February." A decades-old tradition at the college and community Valentine's Day party was for couples moving into courtship or a betrothal to dance to 'Let Me Call You Sweetheart.' For most of her life, Doro had never figured she would be one of those dancers, and she almost hadn't been because a snowstorm descended on the area that day. Ev had needed to go into the city for a meeting related to a case from the previous year. Heavy snow and gusty winds had nearly ruined the night for Doro. But Ev had gone out of his way to get back in time to escort her to the party, and he had brought a special gift, a vintage Valentine that was a Banyon family heirloom. Picking it up from her grandmother had added to his trek home, but he had done it. For Doro. The memory filled her heart with joy, but she relentlessly brought her mind back to the present. "My point is that most of us have felt left out or not good enough at some point in our pasts, and showing up people who looked down on us can be satisfying. That's especially true if we don't sink to their level. Instead, we're just our new selves, and they realize it."

For a moment, Aggie gazed into the distance. When she looked back, she nodded. "Exactly. I don't want to hurt Rud or make him feel bad. I just want him to see me as the successful, happy woman that I am now, not the unsure, awkward coed that I was."

"Exactly and, even if he doesn't see you with Wade today, he'll take note of your ring."

Aggie lifted her left hand. A small emerald cut diamond winked brightly in its gold setting. "I told Wade that a wedding band was enough. I didn't need a betrothal ring, but he insisted. At least, he didn't spend too much. Besides, Wade made good money working security on the railroad, and he tucked all the extra away. His salary as constable is enough for us to live on, but I'll keep working until..." Her voice trailed off as crimson bloomed in her cheeks.

Doro finished the sentence for her. "Until you have a baby."

"Yes, but first comes marriage," Aggie, her face flushed, said. "And right now, I need to get ready, or we'll be late."

پهگ

An hour later, Doro and Aggie sat at the welcome table set up in the main entrance of College Hall. During the first twenty minutes, a dozen alumni had registered, been given informational packets, and gone on to the rooms reserved for them in either the male or female faculty housing. Some visitors would lodge at Michaw's only hotel, but others preferred to relive old times by staying on campus. By moving some professors around, that group was easily accommodated in Maple Hall, where male faculty members lived, and Wheaton Hall, which was for women professors.

When they were left alone, Doro turned to her friend. "I'm surprised at how many people already arrived. We're expecting more than seventy guests, but only fifteen wrote that they planned to come this morning. Most will be here this afternoon. Or so they said."

"It doesn't matter what time people come," Aggie murmured.

While what her friend said was valid, Doro wished Rud would show up before she and Aggie left their current post. The initial meeting might be uncomfortable. Right now, they had a good vantage point to see young Dr. Ingram before he noticed them. That was an advantage for Aggie, which she deserved. Before Doro could respond, Wade walked into the building. A smile lit his face as he approached the table.

"Good morning," the constable said. Both Aggie and Doro responded in kind before he continued. "When you two finish, Ev and I would like to take you to lunch."

"When did you see Ev?" Doro asked.

Wade turned to Doro. "We just had a meeting with President Adams and a few professors. No one expects trouble this weekend, but keeping the rare manuscript safe is a concern. So are possible pranks by fraternity pledges." He rolled his eyes. "There are always a few who cross the line, but Ev and I are concerned the big event will give them more ideas and more places to stage their stunts."

Since she and Ev had already discussed the issue, Doro nodded. "Were the faculty members present at the meeting also advisors to fraternities?"

"Yep," Wade replied. "They already told the houses to keep pledges in line, and to be good examples."

"It's been a while since anything really outrageous happened," Aggie put in. "President Adams has done a good job of convincing the fraternities not to encourage bad behavior."

"He has," Doro agreed. "After the window-soaping episode uptown a few years ago, he made all the fraternity boys take part in the clean-up."

A wry chuckle escaped Wade. "It was a good lesson. However, the last couple of years, they took their antics into the city. President Adams didn't like them going to speakeasies and said so."

"At least none of them drank too much," Doro added. "Since Mr. Fulton was murdered last summer, word has spread that bootleggers can be violent." The local man had gotten involved with two rival bootlegging gangs, which led to his demise.

"That was a sobering event, in more ways than one," Wade observed. "Many folks, not just students, learned a lesson as far as speakeasies and bootleggers. That won't completely end antics from pledges, though."

Briefly, Doro considered the history of fraternities at the college. For the most part, their hijinks had been harmless. "When I was a little girl, and before the window-soaping and speakeasy forays, their pranks were usually played on each other. Taking a fraternity sign down and replacing it with the emblem of another house. Putting bells on every limb of the trees around a house, especially when it was windy. That worked a few times, since spring weather almost always brings a lot of gusty days."

"But that's harmless," Aggie said. "Remember, when we were students and one house built a wall in front of the doors of every other fraternity? Then, they drove by honking and yelling. It was in the middle of the night, and the boys couldn't get out, so they started pouring from the windows."

A frown creased Wade's forehead. "That could've been dangerous. What if one of the houses had caught fire?"

"That's why the pranksters had to spend the rest of the night taking down the walls," Aggie told him.

"I was still working on the railroad, so I don't remember," Wade said.

"You were lucky," Doro commented. "We didn't have a campus security officer, so the town constable helped by overseeing the wall removal. He wasn't pleased to be awoken for a campus issue."

Wade nodded. "When I took the job, I was told covering the campus was part of my responsibilities. Luckily, the flagpole sitting rage was the main issue I dealt with. That went on for two years. The fraternities competed to see whose member could stay up the longest."

Laughter left both Aggie and Doro. "Then, President Adams said he'd have all their flagpoles taken down, if it happened again," Doro said.

"He was worried one of them would fall and get seriously hurt," Aggie pointed out.

"A valid concern," Doro said. "Which is the same reason the door to the bell tower in College Hall stays locked and has for years. One year, pledges went out on the ledge and draped a banner there."

"The door was kept locked right after that," Aggie said, "but getting a key wasn't impossible. Luckily, it's harder now."

The glint in her friend's gaze ignited the memory of how the pair had met. Doro was about to comment when Wade spoke again.

"I'm glad it is, because it's one less thing to consider," Wade murmured.

"The Smith family won't arrive until later," Doro asked. "With the manuscript."

"I know," Wade replied. "Ev mentioned you being concerned about security for it. We asked President Adams about the Smiths' planned arrival and where they were taking the book when they get here. Mrs. Jones already made arrangements for them to come straight to his office. He expects them this afternoon."

The President's secretary, who was also an old and dear friend of Doro's mother, was proficient and professional. "Mrs. Jones started to say something about special guests after our committee meeting yesterday morning, but someone interrupted."

"Mrs. Jones had to get to the office," Aggie put in. "I'm sure she planned to tell you about when the Smiths are coming."

"Most likely," Doro agreed. "She has to be at least as busy as we are, maybe busier since many visitors will call or stop at the President's office. Some will want to see her. Before she became the president's secretary, Mrs. Jones was active on campus as a faculty wife. Welcoming alumni comes naturally to her. She'll take care of the Smiths, although I wish she'd get more of a break before tonight's dinner. People can come and mingle at six-thirty. That won't give her much time to freshen up and get to the auditorium."

"Busy days." Wade again focused on Aggie. "So, what about lunch?"

After a glance at her watch, Aggie nodded. "We have to stay until twelve-thirty, but we could meet you and Ev after that."

Before Wade replied, another man stopped at the table. "I hoped you'd have lunch with me, Ag."

Something between surprise and dismay grabbed Doro when she looked at the newcomer. Beside her, Aggie stiffened. A glance revealed that the color had left her face, making her freckles stand out. Doro laid a reassuring hand on her friend's forearm.

Chapter Three

"Don't tell me I've changed so much that you don't recognize me, Ag," the young man said.

"Of course, I know who you are," Aggie murmured.

Doro did, too, because Rudyard Ingram looked almost the same as he had the day of his college graduation. Lanky and lean, with his dark auburn hair clipped close, he had aged very little. Only a few fine lines radiating out from his brown eyes gave testament to the passage of time.

His eyes glittered as he studied Aggie. "I'd recognize you any place, although your clothes are more fashionable and your bob is stylish, but I miss your braid."

"I cut my hair years ago," Aggie observed.

"I know, and it's a shame," he replied. His expression grew solemn. "A lot is too bad about what happened years ago. I thought of writing after my parents died last year. My father had health trouble for a while, and caring for him was a burden to my mother. She passed not long after him."

Both Doro and Aggie expressed their condolences.

"Thanks," Rud said. "I've had my hands full since then. Running the whole practice alone kept me busy, and there was the estate to settle. That's not quite done, but now, I'm in a better place, which is why I wanted to come back to Michaw and see you." His attention remained on Aggie.

Wade cleared his throat. "I don't believe we've met."

A puzzled expression blanketed Rudyard's face as he looked at the constable. As usual, Wade was clad in his uniform, and Rud surveyed the other man from head to foot. "With luck, we won't become acquainted on a professional basis, since I don't make it a habit to do wrong." After a wink at Aggie, he went on. "I only committed one misdeed during my college career, and that was with this lovely young lady."

As Doro glanced from Wade to Aggie, she saw the former looked uneasy while the latter was dismayed. In an attempt to soothe possibly roiling waters, Doro jumped into the conversation. "Wade knows about the mystery of the lost exam. We've discussed it in the past, since it's how Aggie and I met."

"And how she and I started court..."

Before Rud could finish the word, Doro interceded. "It was your last year of school. As I recall, you were focused on your studies, so you could go to medical college." Although she recalled no such thing, Doro didn't want the young doctor mis-characterizing his relationship with her best friend. As Aggie had said, their college connection was in the distant past, and it had not been a courtship.

He grinned before continuing. "We stepped out fairly often." Rud focused on Aggie, who looked more and more discomfited.

Anger simmered inside Doro at the young doctor's machinations. How dare he put Aggie in an uncomfortable position? And why?

"Stepped out." Wade echoed the phrase as he focused on his betrothed. "I thought you two were casual acquaintances."

A chuckle left Rudyard. "Not so casual. Unfortunately, we couldn't move from stepping out to courting due to outside influences."

From her peripheral vision, Doro saw Wade clench his fists. Although the constable had a jovial demeanor, he clearly did not like what he was hearing. And who could blame him?

"We never really formally stepped out, Rud," Aggie said. "We took in a few movies in Sylvania and attended some campus events, although never when your family came. We were fellow students over a decade ago, and we went places and did things with others in our classes. Nothing more."

"I'd rather not discuss personal matters in public," the young doctor said with another wink.

"We don't have personal matters," Aggie insisted, "and anything you want to say will be shared with Wade anyhow."

Rud jerked a thumb at the constable. "Why is it this guy's business?"

"Because we're engaged," Wade muttered.

Shock slackened Rud's jaw. "What? You're old enough to be her father."

Wade went red in the face, but Aggie jumped to her feet and put her fisted hands on her hips. "He is not, although it wouldn't be your concern if he was."

"Sorry," Rud muttered. When he reached across the table to take Aggie's hand, she pulled back but he did not release her. "Come on, Ag. Surely, you're free to talk with other men."

"I'd be free if you took your hand off me," she murmured.

Wade grabbed Rudyard's forearm. "Let her go."

The harshness in Wade's voice stunned Doro, who had known the constable all of her life. Never had she seen him anything but calm. Now, anger glittered in his eyes, but he was reacting to Aggie's distress, so Doro did not fault him. She wanted to calm troubled waters, though. Wade looked ready to punch Ingram, and that would only create more of a scene. "Rud, I remember you as sometimes being high-handed, but not rude or overbearing."

The doctor removed his grip and stepped back. A rueful expression blanketed his face. "I was too full of myself years ago, but I've grown up. I meant no harm or disrespect, but I only came this weekend because of you, Ag." He glanced from her to Wade and back. "I don't want to step out of line. It's just that you two are a rather odd couple. The age difference, and a constable doesn't usually have an advanced degree while Ag is a professor and a poet."

Rud's mild tone and casual demeanor should have sapped any judgment from his assertion, but a glance at Wade revealed he felt the sting of criticism. Doro filled in the awkward moment. "Why don't we get you signed in? Then, you can seek out your lodgings." She shuffled through the papers in front of her. "I see you're staying in the faculty men's residence."

"I am," he replied. "It's kind of the college to offer free lodging to alumni."

As chairwoman of the planning committee, Doro had suggested the idea. Many people, graduates and former employees, had been affected by last October's crash, which meant they might not be able to afford both travel and accommodations. But Rud came from a wealthy family. Surely, he could pay for a room. "Your lodging won't be as comfortable as a room at the Main Street Inn, but I suppose there are no vacancies at the hotel."

A half-shrug pulled up one of Rud's shoulders. "I didn't call there. A free space is better than paying. Besides, I'd like to stay on campus for the most part." Once again, he smiled at Aggie. "I hope we can renew our old friendship."

As Wade's jaw tightened, he stared at the younger man. Doro silently urged the constable to remain composed.

"Here is your packet with information, Rud," Doro said. "Someone at Maple Hall will direct you to your room. Not much is happening this early, but you might enjoy walking around campus or down Main Street."

The young doctor turned back to Aggie. "Going into town—such as it is—doesn't interest me."

After Rud took a few backward steps, Doro noticed his attire was not as stylish as it had been when they were college students. His outfit, except for his highly polished brown two-tone wingtips, showed wear. Perhaps, he had chosen something old for the trip, although that seemed odd. Many wealthy men still wore driving coats to protect their clothing while on the open road. Doro recalled Rudyard having winter and summer dusters. "Did you drive up from your home?" she asked.

"No, he didn't," another male voice put in. "He took the train to Sylvania. We both did, and we shared a ride from there. The young man who brought us needed to be paid, of course, so Rud owes me his half."

Dark color surged into Rud's face. "I'll pay you after I get settled and unpack."

Since any ride from the nearby town would be inexpensive, Doro again felt surprised, but she returned to her duties. "Welcome back to Michaw," she said to the new arrival. "We have a list of activities for everyone."

A grin split his handsome face. "You don't recognize me, Doro."

She took a closer look. "Lester. Lester Jonson." Doro stood up and extended her hand.

His larger one closed around hers. "Yep. It's good to see you again."

"It's wonderful to see you, too," Doro said with genuine enthusiasm. Despite the passage of a nearly a decade, he looked much the same as he had during their college years. Sturdily built with wavy brown hair and light hazel eyes, he was a good-looking young man. "When I read your note about coming, I was hoping your sister would attend, too."

His smile wavered. "I couldn't talk her into it."

"Because she has better sense than you," Rud murmured. "Juliet must realize plenty of people remember your larceny."

Lester's nostrils flared with a sharp intake of breath as he spun to face the other man. "Plenty of people, Rud? Unless you blabbed, or plan to blab, only a handful know about a foolish choice by two youngsters. Before I decided to come this weekend, I corresponded with President Adams, who sent a warm welcome for my sister and me."

A harrumph left Rud. "He was foolish in letting you and Juliet off the hook."

"But that's not your business, is it?" Wade asked.

Rud's lips flattened. "As a constable, you agree with stealing?"

A flush covered Wade's face. "Of course, I don't."

When Wade took a step toward Rud, Aggie addressed the doctor. "You should go to the faculty residence hall and unpack. Lunch will be served soon, and you can eat there."

"That's a wonderful idea," Doro said.

For a moment, Rud looked like he would object. Then, he nodded. "It was a tedious trip, and I could use some peace and quiet." He reached into his jacket pocket and extracted an envelope. "I planned to send this before I came, but I second-guessed myself. I still hope you'll read it." He handed the missive to Aggie before turning and striding away.

When Rud was out of sight, Wade released a long breath before looking at Aggie. "You feeling all right?"

She smiled. "Of course, and don't let anything Rud said bother you."

"Rud always had a certain air about him," Lester observed.

Doro considered the observation. "I suppose he did," she murmured, "although he was usually pleasant and polite." Memories niggled on the edges of her mind. Usually but not always. Before her recollections took shape, the conversation moved on.

"To you, because your dad was a professor," Lester commented, "and to Aggie, because you two girls became best friends."

The response gave Doro pause. Perhaps, she had not known Rud as well as she had figured. Aggie's earlier revelations pointed to that. Now, Lester's comments supported the idea. And Rud had been part of a group of three upperclassmen who had teased her. As vague memories rose, she made an observation. "Rud hasn't come to mind in years."

"No, he certainly hasn't." Although Aggie addressed Doro's remarks, she focused on Wade.

The constable smiled. "Good to know."

Doro felt a surge of relief when Aggie grinned. After a moment, she gathered her wits and again spoke to Lester. "You're also staying in the men's faculty residence, right?"

"Yep. I've never been inside there, and I'm curious about the place," he replied. "Maybe someday, I'll be a professor myself. It's always been my dream. You two are lucky to have achieved that status."

The note of envy in his voice bothered Doro, but she ignored it and commented on the rest of his statement. "I haven't been past the front hall, since ladies are only allowed there, but I hear the apartments are similar to those in Wheaton Hall. Not luxurious but comfortable."

"Comfort is all I ask," Lester said.

"I can walk you over," Wade suggested after introducing himself.

"Thanks," Lester replied.

After Doro handed a welcome packet to Lester, Wade turned back to Aggie. "So, will I see you at the diner?'

"Absolutely. I'll look forward to it," she replied. "We'll wrap up here and be there around one o'clock."

"I'll be there, too," Doro added.

"Ev will be glad of that," Wade said before he and Lester headed out.

Doro would be more than glad to spend time with her sweetheart, her best friend and Aggie's betrothed. An hour of casual conversation would be good for all of them.

ϟ

Shortly after twelve-thirty, the two friends were on their way to the diner. When they passed the Main Street Inn, Doro and Aggie ran into a couple just stepping out of the hotel.

"Hello, girls. It's good to see you two again." The man's green eyes glittered with warmth.

When she recognized one of her classmates, Doro grinned. "Hank Devlin. It's wonderful you came this year." Her gaze went to the woman beside him. Although Doro was relatively tall, this lady had her by several inches. In fact, she was nearly the same height as Hank.

"My wife and I decided to get away while her folks could watch our kids," he replied. With a nod to the women, he went on. "This is Mrs. Cereta Devlin."

"How do you do," his wife said in a formal tone, which matched her style of dress. The woman could have stepped out of pre-Great War America when ladies wore ankle-length skirts and kept their hair long but contained in a braid or bun. Mrs. Devlin sported the latter.

After they all exchanged greetings, Hank turned back to Doro. "The last time I came for Founder's Day, you were getting your master's degree in Ann Arbor. Aggie was, too."

"We had planned to come that year, but she was tied up judging a poetry contest for high school students, so I stayed and helped with logistics. It's the only year I've ever missed," Doro observed. "You must be busy, since you haven't come on a regular basis."

He nodded. "Practicing medicine is time-consuming, but I love it."

The comment jarred Doro's memory. "I recall you majoring in science, but I was surprised when I saw that you're a physician. Weren't you going to the veterinary school where your uncle taught?"

His lips flattened. "I was, but it didn't re-open after the war like he figured. Other small vet schools closed, too. My uncle opened a private practice, but business wasn't enough to support two vets. He suggested I try for medical school, so I did. Mostly, I enjoy treating people, and my family and I have two dogs, four cats, two goats, two horses, and a pony." A grin lit his face. "I treat all of them myself."

Both Aggie and Doro chuckled. "You obviously didn't settle in the city," Aggie said.

"No. I live about an hour south of Toledo in a small town. On the outskirts of town, really. That way, we have space for all the kids and critters," Hank replied. As he spoke, his wife slid her hand into the crook of his arm.

"How many children do you have, Mrs. Devlin?" Doro asked.

The woman blinked rapidly, as if she was surprised at being addressed. "Four. Two boys and two girls."

"What a lovely family," Aggie remarked.

"I'm a lucky man." Hank glanced at his wife, who was his opposite in coloring. Dark brown hair and almost black eyes provided a distinct contrast to Hank's fair complexion and straw-yellow hair. "Cereta's parents were able to stay with the children and critters this year. Her father is a farmer, so spring and fall, when the alumni events take place, have never been a good time for them to help us out. Unfortunately, he had a heart attack last winter and is leasing out his property this year."

Both Doro and Aggie expressed their sorrow and the hope that Mrs. Devlin's father recuperated.

The woman sighed. "Hank doesn't think Pa should go back to farming, but selling the place isn't feasible now. Not after the crash."

"Maybe things will get better soon," Aggie suggested. "At least you have someone to rent it."

"Yes, I suppose we're luckier than many in that way," Mrs. Devlin murmured, but her bleak expression did not match her words.

Doro smiled. "I'm happy you could come. Hank, you're bound to see some of our classmates, as well as your fraternity brothers. Maybe you have already. You aren't the only doctor among the alumni, although a few were in classes ahead of or behind ours. You remember Rud Ingram."

"I'm sure Hank does," Aggie said with a smile. "He was your big brother in the fraternity, right?"

All good humor left Hank's countenance, while his wife looked equally displeased. "Yep."

His wife gripped his arm tighter, but said nothing.

Their reaction confused Doro. "Have you crossed paths with him over the years?"

Hank's expression went from fixed to forlorn. "We live only two miles away from his hometown, so I see many of his former patients."

"That's been going on since Rud's father got sick, which makes a lot of extra work for my husband," his wife put in. "It's worse now. At least there's a man on the place when Hank makes emergency calls at night. Despite his heart trouble, my father is a better shot than I am, and everyone in the area knows it. Having him with us makes me rest easier."

The observation brought a question to Doro's mind and lips. "Have you had much crime?" She knew most farmers kept a shotgun handy. Often, it was to scare foxes from a henhouse. Occasionally, a vagabond slept in a barn without permission. Would Hank's wife shoot people or critters?

"Of course not," Hank hurried to reply. "Having weapons is pretty common out in the country. I don't hunt but many do."

"That's right," his wife agreed. "Now, if you'll excuse us, we want to take a walk so I can see some of the campus."

"Of course," Doro replied, but the words were barely out of her mouth when the couple strode away. As soon as they were out of earshot, she turned to her friend. "Why did Hank refer to people as Rud's former patients?"

"Good question," Aggie said. "But they didn't want to talk more."

"They certainly didn't," Doro agreed. "Let's get to the diner. We're already late in meeting our fellas."

Within moments, Doro and Aggie entered the restaurant to find Ev and Wade seated in a booth at the back. The lunch crowd had thinned out, so their table was somewhat secluded. Both men smiled and rose as the two friends approached. After exchanging greetings, they all sat down, with the couples across from each other.

"You look worn out," Ev said to Doro.

A half-smile tugged at one corner of her mouth. "You're a sweet talker, Everett Mallow."

He chuckled before his expression grew pensive. "I'm worried about you taking on so much. Teaching two classes, your full-time job in the library, and being chairwoman for this weekend's big events. Not to mention you're still the faculty advisor to that young women's group, and you want to polish your book. It's a lot on your shoulders."

"It is," Aggie chimed in before Doro could respond. "The committee helped with the weekend festivities, but the big burden is on Doro."

"You and Mrs. Jones have done far more than the others," Doro told her friend. "I appreciate it." She turned to Ev. "In three days, it'll be over. In another month, the school year ends. After that, I'll have plenty of time to relax and polish my manuscript."

For a moment, Ev studied her face. "All true, but I don't want you getting sick in the meantime."

"I won't," she assured him. To move talk away from herself, Doro addressed the constable. "Did Lester get settled?"

"Yep," Wade said. "Professor Harlow was returning from class, and he escorted Lester, who was in a couple of his classes years ago, up to the room. They're sharing, since there were more visitors wanting lodgings on campus than could be accommodated, even with professors shifting around."

"Lester majored in history, which is what the professor teaches," Doro said.

"Like your dad," Aggie put in.

Doro nodded. "Professor Harlow and Dad were colleagues for years, and they correspond," Doro replied. "I'm glad Lester ran into him. They'll enjoy catching up."

"They already did a little," Wade said.

The edge in his voice unleased curiosity in Doro. "How so?"

After a glance at Aggie, the constable responded. "Harlow mentioned being surprised Rudyard Ingram returned for a visit. The professor saw him earlier."

"Why was Harlow surprised?" Aggie posed the question.

Wade, his expression solemn, laid his hand over hers. "I know you spent time with Ingram, and he helped save your scholarship."

A frown furrowed Aggie's forehead. "Rud was nice to me, when I needed that. But we weren't really sweethearts, which I realized when he graduated and cut ties with me." She looked around the group before focusing on Wade. "Like I told you last evening, my feelings for Rud were a pale imitation of how I feel about you."

Her fiancé gently squeezed her fingers. "God rest my first wife, but I feel the same way."

Aggie offered a soft smile. "I was lonely, and it made me feel good that a popular boy like Rud wanted to spend time with me. Maybe I thought we'd be more than friends, but we weren't suited and his mother made that clear."

Doro searched her memory. "When she came for his graduation?"

"Yes." Aggie swallowed hard. "It doesn't matter now, and it hasn't mattered for a long time."

"What did she say?" Wade asked.

Aggie clasped his hand tighter. "It's embarrassing."

"You don't have to talk about it in front of me," Ev said.

Aggie's hazel eyes widened as she focused on him. "Everett Mallow, Doro is like a sister to me, and you're like a brother."

A grin touched his lips. "Glad to hear that, because I love you like my own sister."

After a deep breath, Aggie spoke again. "Rud had invited me to visit that summer. When I thanked his mother for the invitation, she was shocked. He tried to cover it up, but Mrs. Ingram made it clear that I wasn't welcome. After all, I'm not their kind of people."

Doro's jaw dropped. "She said that?"

Aggie nodded.

Wade released Aggie's hand and put his arm around her shoulders. "Nasty snob."

"That's for sure," Ev said. "What an awful woman. You're too good for him and his family."

"That's right. You most certainly are." Doro reached across the table to take her friend's hand. "Far too good."

"You're a treasure," Wade said.

"Thank you. All of you," Aggie murmured. For a moment, she let her head rest on Wade's shoulder.

Watching them, Doro experienced a wave of emotion that blotted out present concerns. Happiness for her friend and hope for herself were among them. Ev clearing his throat drew her focus.

"I don't want to pry, but how did Ingram act today?" Ev asked.

"Friendly," Aggie replied before sharing what had happened.

"More than friendly," Wade added. "He wants to renew their relationship."

Aggie pursed her lips. "There's nothing to renew. Not really, and now, you understand why."

Wade's gaze narrowed. "Not on your part maybe, but he made it clear he came to reconcile. Isn't that what was in the letter?" Once again, the constable's voice held a sharp edge.

"I haven't had time to read it," Aggie said, "and I'm not in a hurry to do so, since nothing he has to say matters to me."

Some of the tension left Wade's expression. "It's private, so read it at your leisure."

"I plan to, but that won't be in the near future," Aggie murmured with a slight grin. "I have more interesting activities planned. Among them are going to the big dinner tonight with my fiancé."

Wade grinned back. "You're too good for him. And for me, too."

Laughter left Aggie. "You and I are perfect for one another."

Although Doro enjoyed seeing her friend and the constable so happy, she wondered what Harlow and Lester had said. "I don't want to meddle, either, but what did you hear between the professor and Lester Jonson?" When a snort of laughter escaped from Ev, Doro scowled. "What's so funny?"

"We all know you love to snoop," he replied with a wink. "Always sleuthing."

Smothered chuckles left both Aggie and Wade. Doro shot quelling looks at them, but they focused on their menus. She pursed her lips. "Only if there's a good reason." When Ev's laugh became a chortle, she pressed on. "If I hadn't snooped in the speakeasy that night last summer, you would've met with those bootleggers in their office and maybe not gotten out." She and Ev had not discussed the situation for months, but it still haunted Doro. After a local bootlegger's murder and the disappearance of his wife, Ev had temporarily returned to the Prohibition Bureau. To identify the killer, he had gone under-cover with a gang, where he'd dropped out of sight. Apprehen-sive about his safety, Doro had convinced Aggie and Wade to go with her to the place Ev had last been seen—a Toledo speakeasy. Relief had filled Doro when she'd seen him, but it had been short-lived after he insisted on meeting with the gang's bosses. She scanned his expression. "You don't agree?"

His expression grew solemn. "I have to admit you're most likely right."

"But you don't want to," Doro murmured.

Ev lightly clasped her fingers. "You're right most of the time. I have no problem admitting it. If I hadn't escorted you outside that night, I might not have walked out at all." His gaze glittered with something akin to amusement. "You could admit you're a curious person."

The warmth of his hand and the sincerity in his gaze made Doro relent. "I admit it." After squeezing his fingers, she focused on Wade. "So, what did they discuss?" Although the other three chuckled, Doro was not put off.

"Professor Harlow mentioned Rudyard Ingram plagiarizing a final paper during his last semester here," Wade said. "He intimated Ingram probably engaged in academic dishonesty before then, as well."

"What?" Aggie sounded as shocked as Doro felt.

"Lester wasn't surprised. Evidently, his sister Juliet knew Ingram paid another student to write the essay, but she wasn't comfortable saying anything," Wade explained.

"I understand why," Aggie said.

"As do I," Doro agreed. "She and Lester had their own problems to handle."

The men exchanged puzzled glances before Wade spoke. "Why wouldn't Lester's sister tell what happened? Professor Harlow seemed to understand, and Lester definitely did, but I don't."

"Neither do I," Ev added. "Why wouldn't she report him?"

A moment passed before Aggie spoke. "Doro and I have talked about how we met."

Wade grinned. "Yep. Ev and I know the story. Aggie was a student worker for an old professor who misplaced his final examination and blamed her. Doro and her dad helped figure it all out." His good humor dissipated. "And Ingram worked with all of you."

Aggie cleared her throat. "There's more to the tale. Doro and I kept quiet about the details because others might've been hurt."

Beside Doro, Ev sat up straighter. "Wade mentioned meeting Rudyard Ingram this morning and some cryptic remark the guy made to Lester Jonson about him and his sister stealing. Wade didn't get it, and neither do I."

Since both Aggie and Wade looked tense, and Ev sounded suspicious, Doro crafted her words with care. "I don't suppose it matters much now, and I know neither of you will repeat what we say." She glanced at Wade before turning back to Ev.

"Of course we won't," Ev assured her.

Wade was slower to agree. "I suppose not."

Aggie clutched his arm. "It was a long time ago, but I don't want Lester or Juliet to be hurt by gossip. I'm sure she didn't come this weekend because she feared that."

Ev took a deep breath. "Maybe you could tell us the details, so we know what's going on."

"Nothing is going on now. At least it shouldn't be," Doro said.

"Why don't you tell them?" Aggie asked. "Your dad was the one who smoothed things over."

"What had to be smoothed over, other than Aggie keeping her student job and her scholarship?" Wade inquired.

"I'd like the details, too," Ev agreed.

Although the incident remained clear in her mind, Doro took a moment to organize her response, mostly because the two men obviously wondered why they had not already heard the entire story. "Only a handful of people knew exactly what happened. Rud, Aggie, and me, of course. The department secretary, Miss Collins, my dad and President Adams. We all agreed to keep the particulars quiet, so as not to hurt Juliet and Lester."

Ev's gray eyes narrowed. "I'm beginning to catch the drift." He focused on Wade. "You mentioned Ingram making a snide remark to Jonson."

"Yep," Wade muttered. "At the welcome table this morning, but Ingram mentioned people knowing about the Jonson siblings engaging in larceny. It didn't make sense earlier. Now, it does."

"Because the examination wasn't misplaced by Professor Folsing, it was stolen by Lester and his sister." Ev focused on Doro as he spoke. "You and Aggie have kept the secret all this time. Did you think Wade or I would reveal it?"

The hurt expression on his handsome face pulled on Doro's heartstrings. "Of course not, but there wasn't a good reason to delve into the issue."

"And we promised Doro's father that we'd keep it to ourselves," Aggie added.

"That's right," Doro agreed as she searched Ev's features. Was he truly upset by her withholding the information? The topic had come up a few times, and they had revealed many parts of the story. Just not the fine details.

Ev and Wade exchanged a long look before both nodded. "Understandable, but could we get the whole story now? Since Ingram seemed to threaten Lester with telling all, I'd like to make sure Ev and I are prepared for possible repercussions," Wade said.

"Repercussions," Aggie echoed. "What would those be?"

Ev laid his hands, palms down, on the table. "Lester could react in a negative way. Maybe by picking a fight with Ingram. I haven't met either one, so I can't gauge the possibility. I only know no one wants to be humiliated with an old misdeed."

"Exactly," Wade said. "And Lester was upset."

"But not angry," Doro pointed out.

"Not yet," Wade replied. "However, Ingram enjoyed needling him."

Doro wondered about the characterization. Rud had not seemed tense until after Lester mentioned that they had split the cost of being driven from Sylvania, but Rud had not paid. "They shared a ride, and Rud hasn't paid his half. Which is odd."

With a sigh, Aggie slumped back in the booth. "It is, but I doubt if there'll be trouble between them."

"I agree, but we'll satisfy their curiosity." Doro took a deep breath and went on. "You two already guessed that Juliet and Lester took the test from Professor Folsing's office. Because Juliet worked for my dad, she was familiar with the layout of the history department. She also knew the lock on one of the windows in Folsing's office was missing, so they didn't have to break in, which worked in their favor as far as penalties."

A harrumph left Ev. "If a bank vault is open, and someone walks in, takes money, and leaves, it's still a crime."

Dismay filled Doro. "To lawmen."

"Which I am," Ev said in a cryptic tone.

"Me, too," Wade added.

"You haven't heard the entire story," Aggie said.

Doro smiled at her friend. "They haven't."

"We're listening, so go ahead," Ev said.

After considering a better way to present the information, Doro did. "A little background should be useful. Professor Folsing was failing mentally. He'd been reprimanded for picking on a couple of students every term. Humiliating them in class, giving their papers poor marks without cause, and making their lives miserable. That's what happened to Lester, who started skipping classes to avoid the bullying. Folsing threatened to fail him for nonattendance, which made matters worse."

"Couldn't Lester have dropped the class and taken a different one?" Wade asked.

"No," Aggie told him. "Lester was a history major, and he needed that particular course. Professor Folsing was the only one who taught it."

"Lester faced pressure from his father, too. The man wanted his son to follow in his footsteps and become a lawyer, but Lester had his heart set on teaching history," Doro explained. "Which he does."

"Because your father interceded in this stolen exam case," Ev observed.

His tone held no indication of whether he disapproved or not. "Dad spoke with President Adams about the situation. At that point, we learned that Mrs. Folsing had been concerned about her husband's change in behavior and his forgetfulness. She took him to the doctor, who diagnosed senility. President Adams suggested retirement, and the professor agreed. He didn't even come back to finish the term. With all that in mind, President Adams and my dad decided to let Juliet graduate and allow Lester to continue. Juliet got a job teaching school here, and Lester met weekly with my dad for a time. He never got in any other trouble. After he graduated, they moved to Toledo."

For a moment, silence descended on the group. "So, only seven of you knew the entire story. You, your dad, Aggie, Lester, Juliet, President Adams and Ingram," Ev said.

"That's right, but Professor Harlow evidently surmised what happened. Maybe a few others did, too," Doro concurred. "Why would Rud bring it up now? I haven't heard anyone else do that. It's so strange that he did."

"He acted strangely overall," Aggie said. "Wanting to renew our acquaintance is odd to me."

"What does he look like, so I'll recognize him?" Ev asked.

Doro provided a brief description. "He used to be dapper, but the way he was dressed..." Her voice trailed off.

"Doctors are usually better clad," Wade said.

Curiosity covered Ev's expression. "What was wrong with his clothes?"

"Nothing exactly," Doro replied. "They were shabby, though. Rudyard used to have new clothes. I never saw him in anything faded or worn. But even with the older clothes, his shoes looked almost brand new. Two-tone brown spectator wingtips."

"I didn't know you paid so much attention to men's footwear," Ev said.

"These stood out in contrast with the rest of his attire," Doro responded.

Wade grinned. "The mark of a good detective. Noticing small inconsistencies."

Ev released Doro's hand to pick up his coffee cup. After a sip, he posited a query. "You said his family was wealthy. Did his parents ever donate money to the college?"

For a moment, Doro considered the question. "Not that I know of."

"If they did, I never heard about it," Aggie added. "Not all rich people share their money."

"True," Ev said. "And Ingram hasn't given funds, either?"

The two young women shook their heads before Doro spoke. "If he or his parents made contributions, I'm sure we'd hear about it. Those who donate are always invited to sit at the President's table during the Founder's Day dinner. The elder Ingrams were never there, and Rud won't be there this evening, either."

"So, no donations from him," Wade observed.

"No," Doro replied.

Wade ran one hand through his hair. "I may be off the mark, but I have a bad feeling about the guy."

"As Aggie's sweetheart? Or as a lawman?" Ev asked with a slight smile.

A long, low breath escaped Wade. "I'm not sure, but I'll get it sorted out."

Ev winked at his friend. "I know you will, but I'm going to make it my business to meet the good doctor. If I get a bad feeling, we'll know it's a lawman thing."

All four chuckled, but Doro's mind was churning. She also had a feeling about Rudyard, and it was as uncertain as Wade's.

Chapter Four

After lunch, and before Doro and Aggie parted with the men in front of the constable's office, Ev hesitated for a few moments.

"I'll make my afternoon rounds in an hour and hope to run into Ingram," he said.

"Are you taking Tee along?" Doro asked. "She loves to jaunt around campus with you."

"I enjoy having her with me. My rounds are more fun with her along, but she wore herself out this morning. With visitors arriving, she got more attention than usual. When we got back to my place, she had water, ate breakfast, and went to her bed."

An image of Tee snoozing came to Doro, who smiled. "Maybe you can keep her for the next couple of days, since I'll be busy with the events. I know you will be at times, too, but she can't be left alone for extended periods. She's an active pup."

"She's still young at only two," Ev agreed.

Wade stepped forward. "Ma would be happy to keep Tee at the boardinghouse for a while. My kids will be there after school, and they love to play with her. They had a lot of fun last summer when the two of you were both away."

While Doro had spent three months with her parents in Colorado, Ev had kept Tee. Then, a consulting position with the Prohibition Bureau, where he had worked prior to coming to Michaw, took him away for a week. The short-term job had eventually led to Ev going undercover with the Bureau. Doro brushed that thought away and focused on Wade's offer. "Tee loves your mother and your children, so that'd be wonderful."

"It'd be good for her, since I'm not sure how often I can get her out," Ev put in.

"Don't worry about it. I'll get Tee from you later, or you can drop her off," Wade said. "Right now, I should go inside, so Colleen can take her lunch."

The mention of his clerk reminded Doro of the girl's plans for fall. "I hope Colleen taking classes won't interfere with her work in the constable's office."

"We've got a good plan in place, and she's grateful to both of you," Wade looked from Doro to Aggie as he spoke, "for helping her get a scholarship. Education is important. I wish I had more."

Aggie linked her arm through Wade's. "You're a highly intelligent man, and you don't need a degree to do your job well."

"That's right," Doro agreed.

Wade's mouth quirked. "Say two people with two degrees each."

Doro rushed to offer more reassurance. "You and Ev are both smart and accomplished. Everyone respects the two of you."

"Dr. Ingram didn't seem to be impressed," Wade muttered.

Aggie tugged on his arm. "Who cares what he thinks or says?"

Since the constable only had a high school diploma, he evidently felt the gap. Doro wanted to say many folks did not even complete grade school, but the comment was unlikely to help.

Ev, whose expression was grim, focused on his friend. "Then, he won't think highly of me, either."

"Why won't he think well of you? You're not only intelligent, you're clever and insightful." Doro grinned at him.

His countenance remained blank. "All I've been is a copper. I graduated from high school, which is hardly on a par with medical or graduate school."

Although Ev had mentioned not going to college in the past, Doro didn't consider it an issue. Did it actually bother him? It shouldn't, but now was not the time to discuss it in detail. "Nevertheless, you're as accomplished as Rud." She did not continue by observing Ev was also much more appealing. He already knew she was in love with him!

A half-smile lifted one corner of his mouth, but Ev had no chance to respond because loud voices coming from in front of the bakery interfered. Doro pivoted to see Rud and Stuart Adler, a tall, broad man of middle years, yelling at one another.

"You got nerve showing up in this town again," Mr. Adler, wrapped in a flour-covered apron, shouted. "You better have brung my money with you. I oughta make you pay for the postage I used over the last decade."

"I have no idea what you're talking about." Rud's voice was firm.

Adler grabbed the young doctor by the lapels. "You know exactly what I mean. You bought an automobile from me only a few weeks before you graduated and promised to pay after your folks came for the ceremony. Said they'd bring cash, but I never saw them, and you took off in a big hurry. I had to find out you left town from your roommate."

After a moment, Rudyard grasped the other man's wrists and tried to step away, but Adler held tight. "Let me go, you oaf."

"Oaf, why you nincompoop. I oughta belt you," the older man said.

As soon as Adler drew back one fist, Ev and Wade raced across the street. The constable put one arm between the pair, while Ev clasped Rudyard's shoulder. Both lawmen spoke in voices that did not carry, much to Doro's dismay. "Let's go over and listen to what's happening," she said to her friend.

Several seconds preceded Aggie's response. "All right."

The two friends hurried across the street but remained several feet away.

"I told you two to calm down, and I meant it," Wade muttered.

His words and expression revealed a host of disgust. Whatever had been said out of the young women's hearing had not helped. Looking from Rudyard to Mr. Adler, Doro wondered if the constable could get through to them without additional confrontation. The older man was furious, while the younger one looked aghast. Since Rud came from a wealthy family, him skipping out on a debt made no sense. While Stu Adler was a curmudgeon, would he concoct an accusation?

"I just want this deadbeat to pay me what he's owed for over ten years," Adler said. "I wrote him many times. I even contacted the constable in his hometown, but the man didn't believe me." He glared at Rudyard. "I'm sure you and your pa lied about you stealing my boy's vehicle." Tears filled Adler's pale blue eyes. "We needed money for my boy's care or we woulda never parted with it."

"I paid you cash," Rud insisted. "All along, you wanted more because my folks had money. And you still want more, but you aren't getting it. I should've never come uptown today."

"Why did you? Didn't you plan to stay on campus?" Doro asked.

Rud glanced at her. "When I unpacked, I realized a couple of items were missing."

Stu Adler made a menacing gesture. "I want my money."

When the baker moved toward Ingram, Ev spoke again. "Please step back, Mr. Adler."

Wade laid a hand on Adler's arm. "Stu, let's see if we can settle this peaceably."

After a nod, Adler released Rudyard and moved away. "He cheated me, Wade, and I been trying to get my money for years. Now, he's here, and I want it."

"Like I said, I paid you in full a decade ago," Rudyard muttered.

Adler took a half-step forward before Wade caught his arm. "Hold on, Stu. I was working on the railroad back then, so I don't have the details, although I recall you selling Sam's vehicle."

A faded memory of Sam Adler rose in Doro's mind. "Sam was gassed during the war, wasn't he?"

His father nodded. "It messed his lungs up pretty bad, and he spent a lot of time at various soldier hospitals. He'd worked hard before going to France and bought a beautiful Stutz Bearcat. It was his pride and joy." A sad smile moved the man's mouth. "I kept it up for him while he was gone. When he came back, Sam was sick too much to work, and he didn't want to be a burden on his ma and me, so he said to sell it. Doing it about broke his heart and mine, too."

A snort left Rudyard. "It was just a car, and I paid plenty for it"

The older man lifted his chin. "I charged a fair price, and you didn't pay at all."

While the men spoke, Doro pictured the sleek, powerful automobile. Seeing Sam Adler, young and handsome, drive around town in the shiny vehicle had turned heads—young Doro's included. Once, he had given her a ride, much to her delight. Sadness filled her as she remembered Sam after the war. Pale and wheezing, he had not done much except sit on his folks' front porch. Even so, parting with his wonderful Stutz had to have been hard. "The car must've had a registration and license, so do you have those, Rud?"

"Are you kidding? I junked it long ago," the young doctor replied.

"Junked it?" Adler echoed. "It was a classic. I've seen a few like it on the road, and they're still worth a fair amount."

"Despite your claims about the car being in great shape, it wasn't," Rudyard insisted.

As Adler again moved toward the younger man, Ev interceded. "We need to get to the bottom of this. How did he get the registration if he didn't pay for the car?"

"Because I was a darn fool, and I trusted him to pay before leaving town," Adler, his expression bleak, murmured.

As Ev and Wade exchanged troubled glances, Doro felt her heart sink. Mr. Adler had no proof of his claim, but he was not known to lie. A glance at Rudyard, who had a smirk on his face, increased her dismay. Over the past years, she had wondered why he never returned to campus and cut off communication with Aggie. Had it been, in part, because of him owing money to the baker?

Wade clapped a hand on one of Adler's broad shoulders. "I'm sorry, Stu, but there's not much Ev and I can do, if you have no written proof. If you had gone to the old constable when it happened, maybe something could've been done."

Adler's head fell forward. "I talked to him, and he contacted the constable in Ingram's hometown. That was after I tried. No help from that man. Paid off by Ingram's folks is my guess."

"That's a lie," Rud muttered.

The older man stared at him with hate blazing in his pale eyes. "You're the liar. I shoulda never took your word, but you were a smooth talker back then." His gaze went over Rudyard. "A smooth talker and a fancy dresser, but not so much of either now."

Color surged into Rud's face. "You're hardly a fashion plate with your shabby apron. As for me, I dressed for the train. Too many folks want the windows open, and I'm not getting my good clothes dusty and dirty."

While Doro had wondered about him wearing old clothes to travel, Rudyard's response revealed he hadn't traveled first class, where he would have had a private compartment—something he had bragged about doing in college before getting a car. That thought brought her back to the issue at hand. "Are you sure about paying Mr. Adler all the money?"

Rud looked askance. "Of course, I am. Didn't you hear what I said?" His voice took on a note of impatience.

Aggie took a step forward. "There's no reason to be cross with Doro."

A contrite expression blanketed Rud. "I'm sorry, Ag. I'm not cross. I'm frustrated. It's so unfair for this man to lie about me, especially after all these years, but wealthy folks are often targets of greedy people. I suppose it'll get worse now that money is tight for some."

Privately, Doro did not see what the stock market crash had to do with Rudyard not paying for a vehicle—one that had been purchased long ago.

When Mr. Adler stepped forward, Wade held him back. "Let's go over to my office, Stu. We can discuss the problem there."

"There's no problem," Rudyard shot back, "and I'm not going to your office. I've done nothing wrong."

Wade scowled at the doctor. "I didn't suggest you come. Just get along and try not to make a spectacle of yourself again."

The constable's tone, words and expression stunned Doro. Wade was not acting like himself, and he hadn't been since he met Rud. What could she do to dampen the problem? Doro had not devised a solution when Aggie spoke.

"I'd like to talk to Colleen before heading back to campus, so I'll go with you," Aggie said to Wade before turning to Mr. Adler. "I also want to find out what I can do for your wife. Since she's ailing, I'm not sure what foods are best, but I'm happy to prepare something special."

The intervention worked wonders. Stuart Adler smiled and nodded. "She loved when you sent jam and biscuits last fall. I don't make either one for the bakery."

"Aggie is a terrific cook," Wade added in a more pleasant tone.

"Thank you." Aggie took Wade's arm before winking at Doro. "I'll catch up with you later."

The trio was only halfway across the street when Rud focused on Doro. "Adler is lying." His tone was plaintive and his expression troubled. "I wouldn't steal a car."

Unsure about which man was telling the truth, Doro kept her expression impassive. "I have to get back to campus, but I'll see you at some of the events."

"I'll walk you," Ev put in.

"Wonderful," Doro replied, not commenting on his prior plan to meet with Wade. The two lawmen could talk later.

Rud's response was to turn on his heel and stalk off. Doro and Ev headed the other way. When they reached the end of the block, she addressed him. "You met Rudyard. What did you think?"

"He got darn snotty with Stu Adler."

"He did, but that would be a normal reaction, if Mr. Adler is wrong."

"I don't know Stu Adler as well as the rest of you, but you and I talked to him during the Frotis murder case. He wasn't at all happy about being a suspect."

Thinking back, Doro agreed. "He was angry and offended."

"But he wasn't guilty of wrongdoing, so it's understandable that he got mad and didn't want to answer questions," Ev put in, "even though I didn't like his attitude."

"Maybe Rud did nothing wrong, either" Doro pointed out. "Although I don't go in the bakery much, we're having them provide desserts for the Saturday night dance. Mrs. Jones worked with Bonnie, his daughter, on the order. Mrs. Adler did the orders until her health deteriorated. Before Bonnie moved back to Michaw, Mr. Adler messed up a few special orders. He brought the wrong items a couple of times. Once, he completely forgot about a party."

Ev set his jaw. "That's not good, but would he forget being paid for an automobile?"

A sigh escaped Doro. "His age could be a factor in his memory."

Ev narrowed his gaze. "You're thinking of that professor who was senile and got confused."

Doro nodded. "Professor Folsing was older than Mr. Adler, but it's possible."

"I suppose. I don't know the man as well as you and Wade, but mostly, I've heard Adler's honest and forthright," Ev observed.

"I've never heard differently," Doro said. "But his son's death and his wife's illness have made him edgy. Maybe that's affected him. Although their youngest daughter Bonnie moved back recently, two adult children left after the influenza pandemic. The Adlers lost a young boy in the first wave, and Sam passed away after a long battle with his lung condition."

"From being gassed during the war," Ev said.

Doro nodded. "As his father said, Sam was in-and-out of veterans' hospitals. The doctors did what they could, but the damage was permanent. It wasn't too long after losing him that Mrs. Adler started having trouble getting around. It's due to rheumatism, and she has bad spells where she hardly gets out of bed. When she has one, her husband doesn't like to leave her alone, so the neighbor checks on her when the store is open, and he paid a girl to cook, clean, and do laundry. I imagine that's taken a financial toll, and it may be why Bonnie is back. She works in the bakery and helps at home, but it all seems to weigh on him. Although I don't see him often, I've noticed that he isn't as jovial as he once was. Not that he was jovial during the Frotis case."

"No, he sure wasn't. He bordered on hostile, but he was a strong suspect. All that would affect any man, but would it make Stu invent a story about not getting paid for the car? Or forget he got paid? That seems like a reach."

When Doro slipped her hand into the crook of his arm, Ev laid his own hand over hers. The gesture provided reassurance and comfort. "I'm not sure, but let's not jump to conclusions about Rud."

He cast a glance her way. "You looked uneasy during that whole exchange. After our lunch discussion, I'm wondering what's on your mind."

A slight smile played across her lips. "Other than all I need to do this weekend?"

He chuckled. "Yep, other than that, because I'm guessing you've donned your amateur sleuth hat."

Doro's lips twitched. "Why would you think that? There's no crime to solve, unless we could prove Rud didn't pay Mr. Adler. And we only heard that accusation a few minutes ago." Despite her words, she was increasingly curious about Dr. Rudyard Ingram. Exactly why, she could not pinpoint.

A thoughtful expression formed on Ev's face. "You and Aggie wondered why Ingram returned after so many years. From the bits I got during lunch, he's interested in renewing his—uh—friendship with her. Right?"

Uneasiness again rose inside Doro. Maybe revealing her anxiety to Ev would help put it in better perspective. "Aggie's admission about what Mrs. Ingram said to her shocked me."

"You didn't know?"

Doro shook her head. "No, I guess she was too embarrassed to admit what Rud's mother said."

"It sure sounded that way, and I understand."

After a moment's consideration, Doro agreed. "I do, too, but I wish she had told me sooner. I'm afraid it's been in the back of her mind for a long time."

Several moments of silence passed before Ev spoke again. "You two share a lot, but some things people want to keep to themselves."

The remark made Doro wonder what Ev might not have told her. Before she could ask, he spoke again.

"You said you didn't often accompany the two of them with other students. Why not?"

Tattered memories filtered through her mind. "Freshmen seldom get into cliques of older students. That's true even now, but it was more common back then. Although Aggie and I roomed together, I didn't get close to other sophomores, let alone upperclassmen." Some recollections grew brighter as she spoke. "Thinking back, Rud was imperious at times, although not in front of Aggie."

Ev stopped and turned toward her. "Imperious to you? In what way?"

Doro shrugged. "When I started college, freshmen were required to wear their beanies at all times. They still are, but for a shorter time. Even when coming uptown, but I didn't bother when I was headed home for some reason or another."

He chuckled. "You've always had a rebellious soul then."

After rolling her eyes and grinning, Doro continued. "Mostly, I forgot when I was in a hurry. Anyhow, Rud caught me several times. Once, he was alone and let me pass. The next times, he was with two fraternity brothers, and they made a big deal out of it."

All humor left his expression. "I've heard about hazing. What did they make you do?" His usually warm baritone took on an icy edge.

She laid a hand on his forearm. "Nothing so terrible that you need to look fierce."

His features remained as unforgiving as stone. "Let me decide how bad it was."

After a moment, Doro released her hold on him and stepped back. "They made me carry their books to-and-from their classes for a couple of weeks. That had me running to get to my own classes on time and made me late more than once."

His jaw remained set in a hard line. "Not a nice way to treat a young lady. Did Ingram make you run his books, too?"

"Oh, yes, and he was the worst, since he made excuses to keep me longer than necessary." She chewed on her lower lip. "Until today, I hadn't thought about that in years."

"What did Aggie think?" Ev asked.

More faded recollections resurfaced. "She had bronchitis the week it started and stayed at my house, instead of the dorm. My grandmother came out from Sylvania to take care of her, because my mother was already in Colorado. Our housekeeper pitched in. We were all worried, because Aggie had a bad case of influenza the previous year. It took another week for her to get back to normal, so I never told her because she needed to focus on getting stronger and catching up with schoolwork. Later in the term, the boys lost interest in teasing me."

With one hand, Ev massaged his forehead. "So, Ingram showed some unflattering ways early on."

"He did, although I didn't recall it until now," Doro agreed. "Looking back, his bossiness is probably what made me avoid going with him, Aggie, and others. That, and maybe being treated poorly because I was a freshman."

Ev gently squeezed her hand before walking on. "I wonder why he helped you two with the case of the lost exam."

Doro could not repress a chuckle. "Maybe to impress my father more than us, although Rud liked Aggie, I'm sure. And it wasn't that much of a case. Nothing like the ones we've worked together. Or I've helped you work on."

"We've worked them together, and you've taken the lead often," he assured her. "Wade and I were flat on our backs during most of last year's poisoning case, and in our last investigation, you saved my life, as you reminded me at lunch."

"Aggie, Wade and Lowery Canton agreed with me about you not going back, too." Canton was a supervisory agent in the Prohibition Bureau and Ev's former boss. Even after getting shot, Ev had wanted to return to his role. Doro repressed a shudder at the memory.

"They did, but your opinion is most important to me, and it was what kept me from going to that private meeting and from resuming my undercover persona. I've hung up my gangster gear until the annual campus Halloween party." Humor laced his tone.

She grinned. "I did the same with my flapper outfit. Since I've worn it to two costume parties and to the speakeasy, I'll find something else for this fall."

His dark brows rose a fraction. "You're not wearing it tonight?"

Doro lightly pushed at his arm. "Certainly not. I bought a special dress for the occasion."

"What you have on is mighty nice."

Pleasure wound through her. "Thank you." She glanced down at her outfit, which was one of her best daytime ensembles. The calf-length black skirt was set off by a short-sleeved gray top with black sailor bow. On her head was a black cloche with a gray band. The headwear allowed the edges of her sleek bob to show. As usual, she wore lace-up shoes with a medium heel. "This is fine for work." Prior to knowing Ev, she would not have considered changing to go out in the evening or being stylish at all. Not that Doro had spent many nights in social settings before he came into her life. She had been a wall-flower—and one who didn't care about style. Now, she strove to look more fashionable, although she still spent little time shopping. Instead, she listened to her grandmother's advice and got in-and-out of stores quickly. More important items were always waiting for her. Especially sleuthing.

A rueful smile touched his lips. "I have a late meeting, so you may have to take me as I am right now. I'd rather not go in my uniform, but I want to get Tee to Mrs. Lammers' boardinghouse. Wade said he'd get the dog, but he's busy. I might be able to change clothes, but I doubt if I can shower and shave."

She would take him any way at all, but it would hardly be la-dylike to say so. Instead, Doro cleared her throat. "Don't worry about gussying up. I'm sure your meeting is more important."

He stood up. "I should get back to the constable's office, so Wade and I can talk about sharing duties over the next few days."

Doro glanced at her watch. "I'm late getting to the library, but I'll see you this evening around six-fifteen. Although the dinner doesn't begin until seven-thirty, people can come to mingle at six-thirty, and I want to be there."

"That time frame will give me a chance to change at least," he said with a smile. "I bet you'll be all spiffed up, so your escort should be, too."

"You always look good." As soon as the words were out, Doro felt the flush of embarrassment rise in her face.

A boyish grin formed on his lips. "So, do you." Ev offered a hand to help her up. "See you just after six."

"I'll be ready. By then, we might both know more." And she hoped the knowledge brought peace, not additional worry.

Chapter Five

By four-thirty, Doro's eyelids were drooping. Accomplishing work tasks proved difficult when alumni kept stopping in the library. Since Michaw was a small school, and Doro had spent most of her life on and around the campus, she knew all of them either well or in passing. Some had not been back to campus for a few years, so hearing their news was interesting but time-consuming. She only wished there were more hours in the day and fewer worries on her mind. Rud, Lester, and the fraternity boys were all possible sources of problems, not to mention that a valuable manuscript was a lure to anyone with larcenous tendencies.

Unfortunately, the gift was a topic of conversation with most alumni. More than a few asked Doro when the manuscript would be on display, which only increased her dread. Although she asked where folks were now living, none resided in the New York area. Was she fretting for nothing? She hoped so, but her sixth sense had provided early warnings in the past.

Instead of taking her usual break with a cup of tea, Doro headed to the welcome area to see how the process was going. With little time, she wanted to avoid more casual conversations with visitors, so Doro exited the library through the storeroom in back. She was about to step outside when male voices reached her.

"Get your hands off me. I'm tired of your harassment, Hank."

She stepped dead in her tracks and listened intently.

"You owe me money, and I'm tired of your excuses," Hank muttered.

Doro's hands flew to her mouth. The voices belonged to Rud Ingram and Hank Devlin. No wonder the latter had not wanted to chat about his former fraternity brother.

"I don't owe you that much, and I'll give it to you when the house sells," Rud shot back.

"You owe me a lot, and you may not sell any time soon. We both know it. I've got a family to feed and clothe. I've got animals in need of care, too. Not only that, Cereta deserves to wear something other than remade dresses, and our kids outgrow their duds every few months," Hank said. "On top of that, our roof is leaking. What you owe me will more than cover the bills, so pay up."

With the utmost care, Doro opened the door a crack. Hank's wife stood off to the side, while the two men were nearly toe-to-toe.

Rud gestured to Hank's shoes. "You've got nice wingtips, so you can't be hurting too badly."

Doro glanced down and saw that the two men had identical footwear brown spectator wingtips.

"They're just alike since you ordered two pairs from our mercantile but could only pay for one. Because I delivered his son, the shopkeeper sold me these at a greatly reduced price."

"He made a mistake. I only ordered one pair."

"That's a lie," Hank said.

"Believe what you want," Rud murmured. "I know the truth."

Cereta stepped forward. "Do you? It doesn't seem that way. We've heard plenty of lies from you over the past two years."

"I'll pay you when I have extra money," Rudyard said.

Hank spoke again. "No, you'll pay now. You owe me more than five-hundred dollars. Hand it over."

The amount had Doro stifling a gasp. Few people earned that much in a month.

"Pay us what you owe, Rud," Cereta demanded.

"I don't have that kind of money on me," the other man protested.

"You don't have it, period, do you?" Hank made his words more statement than question. "If you weren't frittering money away in speakeasies, you could pay us in full."

"Like I said, I'll have it when the house sells," Rud insisted.

"Since the crash, few people can buy a home. I want my money no later than the first of the month. If I don't get it, you'll regret it." Hank's voice was rough with anger.

"You most certainly will," his wife agreed.

"Big talk," Rud muttered.

"It won't be all talk if you don't pay up," Hank maintained. "Maybe you're afraid of gangsters, so you pay them what they're owed. But you need to be afraid of me, because I'll do whatever's necessary to take care of my family."

"Aren't patients paying you?" Rud inquired.

"You know most of them are hard up, and it's been worse since Black Tuesday. I have to take eggs, bread, and produce most of the time. If I get anything at all," Hank said.

"At least you've got some food," Rud observed.

"But not enough," Cereta put in. "You took off for the city and left Hank holding the bag. You owed him money then, and you owe more now. What happened to your Stutz Bearcat? You didn't drive here from what we heard."

"I had more pressing debts, and there was no money left after the sale," Rud replied. "Like I said, I'll pay you in full as soon as I can." Within seconds, footsteps faded away.

Doro pressed one eye to the crack and saw Rud hurry off.

Soft sobs followed. "Honey, don't cry. I'll get him to pay somehow. I promise you that," Hank said.

A better peek out the door revealed Hank pulling his wife close and patting her back. Doro blinked back tears. Although the Devlins had been furious, they had a right. Five hundred was a tidy sum.

"I hope you do, because we can't manage much longer," Cereta said in a barely audible voice.

Doro watched as the couple walked away. Rud had multiple debts. Was he desperate enough to go for the rare book? Although Doro was not sure, she planned to share the news with Ev, Aggie, and Wade. Forewarned was forearmed.

After a quick stop at the welcome area in College Hall, Doro made her way back to the library. She did not see her best friend approaching until Aggie spoke.

"You look lost in thought." Aggie's voice cut into her reverie.

"Not lost, but searching."

Her friend's lips quirked. "For what?"

"Let's sit down on one of the benches near the dormitory, and I'll tell you what I overheard."

After the two friends were settled in a private nook away from the main pathways, Aggie gestured for Doro to keep going. "What's up?"

Following a summary of what she had heard, Doro queried her friend. "Rud may be in debt to two people and to gangsters, as well as Mr. Adler."

Aggie rubbed her chin. "No wonder Hank and his wife were terse earlier."

"It sounded like Rud has gambling debts, which is possible if he goes to speakeasies. From what I overheard, Hank has been taking his patients for a long while, and they might've had some sort of deal that Rud backed out of," Doro said.

"Sounds that way," Aggie murmured. "Times are tough everywhere. I've heard freshmen applications are way down, so we may not have as many students in the fall. A few in my classes are worried they can't return."

"I've heard the same things. I hope the situation improves soon. A lot of folks are struggling." Doro released a pent-up breath. "Hank and his family seem to be among them."

"You love a mystery, so are you digging into why Rud seems to be deeply in debt." Aggie's hazel gaze sparkled.

"It's bad enough that Ev teases me about *always sleuthing*, but my best friend joining in is too much." Doro feigned a scowl before it dissolved into a grin. "I don't have time to dig into Rud's problems. I'm just glad the confrontation was in private."

"Me, too," Aggie agreed.

An idea that had percolated in the back of Doro's mind surfaced. "Don't let yourself be alone with Rud, all right?"

Dismay clouded Aggie's hazel eyes. "Do you think he's dangerous?"

"Not dangerous, but desperate. He might try to get you in a compromising position."

Aggie's mouth fell open. "I don't think he'd hurt me."

"Neither do I, but if you're found alone with him, it wouldn't look good." Doro did not point out Aggie's bid for tenure might be hampered by such an event. Or that townsfolk could protest, especially the handful who objected to their constable marrying a younger woman, and a professional one.

"What good would it do to compromise me?"

"You got a nice monetary prize from the poetry contest, and your book sold, so royalties will come in soon. Both were announced in the last alumni bulletin."

One hand flew to Aggie's mouth. "You think Rud is interested in my money."

"Not only the money, since he always liked you," Doro insisted.

Before replying, Aggie looked into her pocketbook, where a paper—Rud's letter—was visible. She pushed it down. "But the prize and book advance would help him pay Hank with some leftover, and Rud mentioned me being a poet when he was at the welcome table."

"I noticed that, too."

Aggie squared her shoulders. "I'll be cautious because Rud isn't getting a dime from me."

"How did Wade's talk with Mr. Adler go?"

"They discussed the car sale. Of course, we didn't know then that Rud recently sold it."

"We can tell Ev and Wade tonight."

"I plan to go to dinner a little early. Ev is picking me up around six-fifteen."

"Wade will come a bit before then, so we'll be early, too. I'd like to see the decorations, and I haven't had time to look. Since the campus has so many forsythia bushes, and they're all in bloom, Mrs. Jones had students gather branches this morning. She and a couple of the other secretaries will put them in vases and place them around the room around five-thirty. She said plenty of tulips are ready for centerpieces, so those were to be made this afternoon."

Talk of decorations was a welcome distraction. "I'm sure it's all in order if Mrs. Jones got involved."

"She was kind to take over that part of the decorating." Aggie grinned. "Her yard probably has enough tulips for most of the tables."

Doro chuckled. "Probably so, and I'm glad she and others are willing to cut them. President Adams wants to be careful about spending money, since we don't know what the future holds."

"It will be a lovely evening. You, Ev, Mrs. Jones, Floyd Quartine, Wade, and I will be at the same table. I know Floyd is your boss, but you two get along well."

Since Aggie had done the seating assignments, Doro had not been sure where she and Ev would end up. She should have known her friend would put them with a congenial group. "Floyd is a terrific boss. I've known him all my life, since he's been the library director as long as I can remember. It should be a wonderful evening. I look forward to it." As they went on their way, Doro hoped the dinner ran smoothly. Another incident involving Rud Ingram would not be welcome. Neither would an outburst from Hank Devlin. With luck, they wouldn't be seated together.

Chapter Six

That evening, when Ev picked her up, Doro noted his tension and wondered what had happened in the past few hours. She did not hesitate to ask as soon as they were outside and walking toward the auditorium. "What's wrong?"

He paused to turn toward her. "I was hoping Mrs. Smith would change her mind about putting the book in the College Hall showcase. President Adams pressed her to keep it in the safe until Sunday afternoon. She didn't agree at all, but he made it clear you didn't ask him to keep trying."

"I'm guessing she mentioned the library director position to him, too. Although he has some say in who will replace Floyd, going against a major patron's wishes would be foolish."

He yawned. "Sorry."

Doro clasped his hand. "Make sure you get some rest tonight, all right? Don't volunteer to take Wade's shift, too."

His eyebrows lifted. "What makes you think I'd do that?"

A chuckle left her. "Because I know you."

He put his free hand up, as if to ward off her comment. "I'll be happy to let Wade take his turn."

"Good," Doro replied. Before the pair started forward again, she shared what she had overheard outside the library.

"Wow," Ev murmured. "So, Ingram is deeply in debt, even after selling the Stutz. I'll tell Wade when I can get a private moment with him. Both Ingram and Devlin bear watching."

By the time they reached the auditorium, Doro felt calmer. The manuscript should be safe overnight, although she hated for Ev and Wade to lose sleep.

Before they entered the room, a soft buzz of voices reached them. "It sounds like more than a few people arrived early," she observed.

"Yep." Ev, who had been holding her hand, released Doro as they stepped inside. "The place looks great."

Doro agreed. The decorations were lovely. Bowls of red and white tulips served as centerpieces on each table, while tall vases of forsythia were placed on short pillars around the room. Low light gave the space a calm, pleasant ambience. The guests were engaged in conversation while soft jazz, provided by a group of music students, played in the background. Tonight's event included a short speech from the college president, the meal, and a concert by Michaw students. The main social gathering, to be held in the same room the next night.

"You look far away," Ev murmured.

Doro turned to see the object of her thoughts. Warmth rushed into her face. "Not so far."

One eyebrow rose. "That's a cryptic reply. Care to share more?"

"Not really."

A chuckle escaped him. "All right. Are you planning to greet people as they arrive or move around and mingle?"

"I'll go around the room until everyone is seated," she replied. "There's a program before we eat. President Adams will give the welcome and introduce my committee. That shouldn't take long."

"Good. I'm starving."

She laughed. "You always are, but usually it's because you skip meals. Today, you had lunch."

"True, but a good dinner is always welcome."

Their conversation went no deeper because Aggie and Wade joined them. "Some of the others on the committee wondered if we're spreading out and informally greeting people. I said you went over that at the last meeting."

"I did, but a few insisted we should have a receiving line. Maybe that affected their listening," Doro replied with a grin. "I'll make my way around the room and reiterate that we're doing informal greetings," Doro said before turning to Ev. "Do you want to go along or would you rather sit at our table?"

"I'll mingle on my own. See you in a few minutes," he replied. "How about you, Wade? Want to go around with me?"

"I'd just as soon sit at our table. We can let our ladies fulfill their responsibilities while we relax." A teasing note entered the constable's deep voice.

"You two should sit down, since you'll each be up half the night," Doro said.

Concern shadowed Aggie's gaze. "Yes, rest now."

The two men shook their heads. "We've both lost sleep before. It won't kill us," Wade pointed out.

"It sure won't," Ev agreed with a laugh.

Aggie chuckled, too, but Doro did not. How could she when the word *kill* echoed in her head. Why, she did not know but odd feelings had risen in her mind in the past...and they had always been meaningful, which meant ignoring them now was impossible.

⁂

For the next thirty minutes, Doro and Aggie welcomed alumni, faculty, and staff. As Doro moved through the growing crowd, she enjoyed seeing familiar faces and exchanging greetings. When people mentioned her parents, Doro touched her throat, where her mother's locket rested. Doro always wore the talisman, which had originally been a gift from her father to her mother. Julia Banyon had passed it on to her daughter before going to Colorado for treatment. How Doro wished her parents were present. If she and Ev wed, would they come for the ceremony? Doro had no time to contemplate the possibility because President Adams called out to her.

"Professor Banyon, please come over," the man said.

Doro quickly scanned the three people with the college president. A couple in their fifties and a young man stood beside the administrator. Although the man and woman were not familiar, the other figure was. Vance Smith had been three years ahead of Doro, and he had been close friends with Rud Ingram. He had also been one of the trio who had harassed her about the beanie, although he had been nicer than the others. "Good evening."

"Good evening," the president said in a pleasant tone that matched his expression. "I want you to meet Mr. and Mrs. Smith and their son, Vance. This is Professor Dorothea Banyon, the chairwoman of the event. She's also one of our librarians, so your rare book will be in her capable hands."

After exchanging greetings, Vance addressed Doro. "We knew each other as students." A grin curved chiseled lips beneath a thin mustache as black as his hair. Pale blue eyes, ringed with ebony lashes, focused on her.

In only seconds, more memories resurfaced. With his good looks and boyish charm, Vance had been popular with his classmates and professors. Not only that, he had been an outstanding student and a fine athlete. Thinking back, Doro could not recall him talking about being wealthy, which he surely was. Had his family given money to the college years ago? If so, she had not made the connection then or more recently, but Smith was a common name. "We did, although I was a lowly freshman, when you were a senior."

"You could never be lowly," he assured her before turning to his parents. "Doro's father was a history professor, and a fine one, so I remember her visiting campus while she was still in high school."

The observation surprised Doro, who did not know how to respond. Vance's father filled the gap.

"My son has an eye for pretty girls, so him noticing you doesn't surprise me one iota." A broad grin lit the face that was, except for some wrinkles, a duplicate of Vance's countenance.

While his black hair was shot with gray, Mr. Smith maintained a youthful grace.

His wife, a petite silver-haired lady, lightly swatted his arm before glancing at Doro. "Both of my menfolk are terrible flirts." The amusement in her voice muted any criticism.

"I see," Doro murmured before restoring her usual aplomb. "I've heard so much about the manuscript, and it is a treasure. I'm sure President Adams has already told you that we'll keep it safely locked in a special glass front case. It will be visible to visitors, but anyone who wants to see it up close will have to go into the library director's office. That will keep it secure."

"Wonderful," Mrs. Smith said. "Having it where all the visitors can see it this weekend is important. The main showcase in College Hall is perfect for that. I'm glad you withdrew your objections, my dear. Very wise."

"It was wise," her husband agreed.

Mrs. Smith smiled. "You might not know, but all three of us are graduates."

"How nice," Doro said. Michaw had been among the first universities in the nation to be co-educational, so Mrs. Smith being an alumnus was not surprising. Neither was her veiled reference to their telephone conversation. Knowing Mr. Smith concurred with his wife only reinforced Doro's decision not to continue her futile objections.

Mrs. Smith glanced at Adams. "We appreciate the overnight security being provided by the local lawmen."

"It doesn't seem necessary," her son put in. "I know a guy who runs an antiquity business back East, and I still don't get why anyone puts stock in old books and stuff."

His mother clucked her tongue. "You have no appreciation for historical artifacts. That book was rare when my grandfather purchased it from his old friend, Percival Derry, and classmate. The passage of time has only increased its value and exceptionalism. It's a first edition of Derry's first book, <u>Traversing the Trillium.</u>"

"We have a copy of the second edition in the library," Doro said. "It isn't rare, because it was popular, so there were many copies. But it's a lovely story about a young man finding his way after fighting in the Civil War."

"I haven't read the tome, and I don't get why the original printing is so valuable," Vance replied, but a grin and a wink took any sting from his words. "I'm a heathen."

Mrs. Smith shook her head. "More of a man about town, but you'll settle down eventually."

His father lightly punched Vance's arm. "No harm in putting your glad rags on and painting the town red. As long as you're staying within the law."

"Of course, I am," Vance assured him.

The exchange made Doro study Vance again. He looked dapper, although his attire was suitable for the occasion. The term *glad rags* evoked images of trendier clothing, the kind worn by speakeasy patrons. Did Vance run with a fast crowd? Doro was about to ask what his occupation was when President Adams interceded.

"I should start the program, so we don't delay dinner," the administrator observed.

After the group exchanged farewells, Doro moved away. A hand on her elbow made her turn back to see Vance grinning again.

"It's wonderful to see you," he said. "I hope we have a chance to talk more before the weekend is over."

His tone had as much entreaty as charm but why? They'd been passing acquaintances a decade ago. Had he really noticed her visits when she was an awkward schoolgirl? Surely, Vance Smith had not harbored a liking for her. "We'll likely cross paths again."

Vance's brow furrowed. "I'd like to do more than that."

Briefly, Doro considered revealing her courtship with Ev, but maybe Vance only wanted to be friendly. Because she was uncertain, Doro shrugged. "As President Adams said, I'm the chairwoman of the Founder's Day events, so I won't have much free time." After a glance at the podium, she continued. "I better get to my table. Enjoy the evening."

Since almost everyone was seated already, Doro had no trouble getting to her own place. All three men—her boss, Wade, and Ev—stood. A round of greetings followed.

After Ev held her chair and the two of them sat down, Doro glanced directly at him. His grim expression caught her off-guard. "Is anything wrong?" she whispered.

For several moments, Ev stared at the head table. When he turned back to Doro, he said, "Young Smith detained you. Talking about by-gone days?"

Because she did not want him getting the wrong idea, she replied carefully. "Not exactly, and we only talked a couple of minutes. We won't have a chance to chat more, so I explained how busy I'll be all weekend."

For a long moment, he studied her face. "He wanted to spend time with you."

"Maybe. I've had more than a few visitors want to chit-chat longer. People like to reminisce about happy memories from simpler times, not that Vance and I share many. None really, except we were both students here, and he might've been in one of my father's classes." Doro realized she wasn't sure about that, either. She was only sure Ev should forget about Vance, as she planned to do. "Any free time I have will be spent with you."

A slow grin took the tension from him. "Good to know."

"What are you two whispering about?" Aggie asked. Amusement filled her voice.

"Nothing," As she looked around the table, Doro noted the smiles on every face. "Nothing in particular."

A chuckle escaped Mrs. Jones, who addressed Doro. "You and Aggie have done a marvelous job, my dear. You planned a wonderful menu. Split pea soup, a fresh salad, roast beef with mashed potatoes, rolls, and green beans. Then, an icebox cake for dessert. I can't wait to try that."

"Doro made one last weekend in the Wheaton Hall kitchen," Aggie put in.

"You did," Ev asked. "How come I didn't get a sample?"

"I planned to bring you a piece, but the entire cake was eaten at a committee meeting," Doro told him. "If you like it, I'll make another one. I got the recipe from Mrs. Fisher, who is in charge of preparing tonight's food."

He winked at her. "Sounds wonderful."

"Maybe you'll share," Wade said, a thread of amusement in his voice.

Ev shrugged. "Maybe."

Although pleased with Ev's reaction, Doro turned back to the older woman. "Thank you, Mrs. Jones. You were instrumental in making the planning run smoothly."

"I only shared what was done in the past," the older woman replied. "You've taken the event to a whole new level. We've celebrated Founder's Day in a big way every five years. With you making this one so special, people will want to come more often for it. Maybe every year."

"It's gracious of you to say so," Doro said, "but you did more than share past plans. You provided guidance on how to avoid problems and raided your garden for the beautiful flowers."

A smile touched Mrs. Jones' mouth. "I've worked on college events for a number of years, and sidestepping trouble is important."

"It certainly is," Floyd Quartine agreed. "Alumni affairs can be especially tricky. Most former students are happy to reconnect with professors and classmates, but a few air age-old grievances. One year a long while back, two young men nearly came to blows because one owed the other money. Or so the claim went."

The comment reminded Doro of Rud, whose debts were concerning. Once again, she wondered why he had come back. Was it to sweet talk Aggie into courting, so he could get her prize money and book royalties? Was he that desperate? Maybe he figured she could keep working if they married, which would never happen. As she looked around the room again, Doro realized Ingram was not present. A combination of relief and disquiet descended over her. What was the man doing? Doro did not have a chance to ponder the question, because conversation continued at the table. But wondering about Rudyard was in the back of her mind. While his absence would keep a confrontation with the Devlins at bay, would he again argue with Mr. Adler? At least the bakery was closed in the evening. Doro chastised herself for such errant thoughts and focused on enjoying her table mates, but Doro never had an opportunity to tell Ev about the exchange between Rud and the Devlins. That required privacy, and they had none. Perhaps, they could talk on the way home. Surely, he had time for that. Nevertheless, she scanned the room looking for Rud Ingram.

"You seem distracted," Ev murmured in her ear.

"Maybe a little," she admitted. "I haven't seen Rud. Have you?"

Ev shook his head. "No, I haven't although I didn't notice until you mentioned it. There's a decent crowd, though. This is my first Founder's Day weekend. Is it a typical number?"

"No. We usually have another few dozen people, and last September, we had that many more interested. When the invitations went out in late February, we received forty letters from people who couldn't come. A few cited business declines after the crash, or their jobs being lost."

"That's happening in many places," Ev said.

"It is," she murmured. "In any case, I want to talk with you. Can you still walk me home?"

"Of course. Wade is taking Aggie home. After that, we'll head to College Hall and talk to the custodians. I'm sure nothing happened, so he'll take the first shift, and I'll handle things after three o'clock."

Their exchange was interrupted by President Adams giving a welcome. Doro and her committee received a round of applause, as did the music students, before the administrator provided the history of the college's founding. When he finished, the soup course was served.

As dinner progressed, some of Doro's tension ebbed. Pleasant banter and good food took precedence. A brief break filled in the gap between the meal and more entertainment by the band and the college choir. After the music ended, dessert was served.

Ev dug in. After a few bites, he turned to her. "I love the ice box cake. It's terrific. I hope you make one for me soon."

"I will," she promised before finishing her own portion. As she did, Doro wondered about expanding her kitchen skills. Sweets pleased Ev, but they were hardly nourishing.

Within minutes, others also wrapped up their meals and began to leave their tables. "We don't need to stay late. In fact, since the meal is over, we could take off any time," Doro observed.

"Probably a good idea. It's already after eleven," he replied before turning to Wade. When the two men finished speaking, Ev addressed Doro. "He and Aggie want to wait a little while before heading out, but we're free to go."

Since people were milling around, Doro and Ev were delayed at points. When they finally made it outside the auditorium, she breathed a sigh of relief before a familiar male voice interrupted.

"Doro, leaving so soon?" Vance asked.

She turned to see him alongside Rud, who wore a fancy pinstripe suit in shades of brown—one suitable for a speakeasy. Her gaze went to his feet, clad in the same wingtips as earlier. Questions about his financial status rose again, but Doro focused on Vance. "It's been a long day."

"I'm sure it has, but you've done a wonderful job as chairwoman," Vance assured her. "The program ran rather long, as did the music at the end, but Rud and I were discussing the great dinner. Weren't we?'

Although Vance looked and sounded sociable, the same could not be said for his friend, who barely nodded in agreement. "Right."

"I'm glad you enjoyed it," Doro said. "Now, if you'll excuse us."

Vance looked at Ev. "Aren't you going to introduce us to your companion?"

Good manners dictated Doro's response. "This is Everett Mallow, our campus security officer and my..." Doro hesitated. Should she say sweetheart? They were courting, after all. Before she settled on proper terminology, Ev spoke.

"Her escort," he supplied.

"And he's not only the campus security officer, he's the deputy town constable," Rud put in.

All lightheartedness left Vance's expression. "You've met him? Surely not because you got in a jam with the law?"

Color surged into Rud's face. "Of course not. He was with Doro and her friends when I was uptown earlier."

"I see," Vance said.

Although the tone of the conversation seemed off, Doro aimed for brightness when she spoke. "Have you two stayed in touch all this time? It's wonderful to keep up with old classmates, especially fraternity brothers."

Almost immediately, Vance again looked casual. "We've seen one another a few times over the years."

"Yep," Rud agreed with a grin.

"How nice," Doro murmured.

"I wish we could stay and talk, but I need to get the professor home and go back to my place soon," Ev said.

Although she did not like him calling her by her title, Doro slipped her hand into the crook of his elbow. "Yes, we should go."

Vance focused on Ev. "President Adams said you and the constable will be guarding my parents' donation overnight. That's going above and beyond the call of duty."

"Not really. It's well within the scope of our duties," Ev replied. "Now, if you'll excuse us."

"Of course," Vance said, a fresh smile firmly in place. "Nice to meet you, Officer. Sweet dreams, Doro."

Beneath her hand, Ev's arm tightened. "Good night," she said and turned away. Once they were farther away from the building, Doro paused. "According to his parents, Vance is a flirt."

When Ev looked down at her, the darkness cloaked his expression, but emotion resonated in his deep voice. "You didn't know that from when you were both students?"

"No, he never bothered with me, except for when he, Rud, and another one of their fraternity brothers caught me without my beanie a few times."

"Did Smith apologize tonight?" Ev asked.

"No. He didn't bring it up, and neither did I." When Ev's hand lightly clasped her shoulder, some of the tension drained from Doro. "None of it matters now."

"Good, but I should get you home before I grab a little sleep."

"Yes, you should," Doro agreed before the pair continued to Wheaton Hall.

Chapter Seven

Only the faintest fingers of light encroached on the darkness outside Doro's bedroom window. Although it was long before her usual time to get up, she rolled out of bed. This was not a typical Saturday morning. More sleep would be a lovely luxury, but checking on Ev was of top importance. Although the plan had been for him to take over at three o'clock, some two-and-a-half hours earlier, she would not be surprised if he had relieved Wade sooner.

After dressing, she made coffee and filled a flask. Since treats were always in the big kitchen on the main floor, Doro stopped there for cookies. She tucked everything into a sack and hurried to College Hall. Because the hour was early, no one was out. As she walked across the empty campus, Doro felt calmer. The book was undoubtedly safe and secure. In a little more than thirty hours, it would be presented to the college and displayed in a more protected location. Everyone would be relieved then. Especially Doro.

When Doro got to the main building, she found the front doors locked. Dismay filled her. She should have thought of that. Of course, it had been secured overnight. No one needed to enter the building then. After putting her bag down, she pounded on the wood. A few moments passed before President Adams, unshaven and disheveled, swung it open. Anxiety clutched at Doro's heart. "Where is Ev?"

"He's fine." After a brief hesitation, the man stepped back. "You might as well come in."

Doro moved ahead of him and into the main hall. A gasp escaped her when she saw the shattered glass in the cabinet doors. "What happened?"

A labored breath left the administrator. "Around two-thirty, the mayor got a call about a fire out at the Little place. The volunteers were headed there, and either Wade or Ev needed to go along. It was bad from what I know. The barn was almost gone when the mayor got the message, so he came over to get Wade after telephoning me. I went to tell Ev. Luckily, he was up and dressed, so we both rushed here." A harsh breath escaped him. "When Ev and I got here, it was the front door was still locked. Then, we found the showcase glass shattered, and the book was gone."

As she looked around, Doro did not see anyone else. "Where are Ev and Wade?" Although she asked about Ev already, the president had not supplied a specific answer.

"Maybe at the constable's office. Ev went there after leaving here around four o'clock. Wade was back by then, and they discussed how to proceed. After that, Wade went home to clean up since he was covered in soot and sweat. He and Ev planned to meet right afterward. By now, they could be out digging up clues."

"I'm sure they are. Do you know if they had any leads to go on?"

"I gave them a couple of hints."

The cryptic comment called for a question. "Like what?"

A weary smile lit his face. "Since you'll undoubtedly get involved in the investigation, it won't hurt to tell you who I saw on my way to get Ev. After all, you're our resident amateur sleuth." His good humor faded. "Hank Devlin was taking a walk."

Surprise hit Doro hard. "By himself?"

"Yep. He said he couldn't sleep and didn't want to bother his wife by tossing and turning. I'm not accusing him of stealing the book, but Ev and Wade will talk with him, since he might've seen someone while he was out. Hank was always as honest as the day is long, so he'd never take anything."

Doro forced herself to remain calm. President Adams did not know the Devlins had money trouble. "You mentioned a couple of tips. What was the other one?"

"Several fellows were walking up from the athletic field. Rather boisterous, so I couldn't help but hear them. Probably fraternity pledges. Because I was in a hurry to get Ev, I only saw them from a distance."

"Maybe Hank saw them. Or even Wade might have when he headed for town."

"Possibly. I'm sure Ev and Wade have already started talking to people. I'll call all the fraternity presidents into my office this morning and find out where their pledges were overnight. I'm not sure they're responsible, but they could be."

His plan made sense because stealing the manuscript would be the biggest pledge prank ever. "That's a wonderful idea. Aggie, Wade, Ev, and I have talked about spring pranks."

Adams wrung his hands. "The fraternities here have taken our guidelines to heart and not done any wild shenanigans for a few years. In any case, I'd like to keep the theft quiet for as long as possible, so Ev and Wade will tell everyone not to spread the word. If we could get it back before the ceremony on Sunday..." His voice trailed off.

"Ev and Wade will do their best," Doro assured him.

"I know they will, but I'll have to tell the Smiths what happened, and I dread that." He glanced at the shattered glass. "After the janitors board up the cabinet, I'll go back to my house. I should have time to clean up before they come downstairs."

"How did the robber get inside? You said the doors were locked when you got here."

"They were," President Adams agreed. "Ev looked all over the area, checked all the outside doors, and around the first-floor rooms, including the lavatories. He was thorough, so even though all the windows were closed, he found one that was unlocked. When Ev looked outside, he could see where branches of the boxwoods were broken, most likely from the thief climbing in and out."

His revelations sent Doro's mind to churning. "The robber could've unlocked the window earlier today," Doro said.

A weary smile touched Adams' mouth. "Ev made the same point."

After a study of the man, Doro offered advice. "Why don't you get some rest? The Smiths aren't apt to wake for a couple of hours. You've been busy all week, and there are still festivities on the schedule. I'm sure Wade will call when they know anything new. Maybe even before the Smiths rise."

The administrator pressed a hand to his forehead. "A good idea. I may not doze off, but lying down sounds lovely."

"I'll go to the constable's office right now."

"Good luck."

"We've been fortunate in other investigations," she replied before going on her way. But none had been solved in a day. That thought dogged Doro's steps as she made her way uptown. Although President Adams didn't want word to get out, people would wonder about the broken glass and boarded showcase. Keeping the missing book secret seemed unlikely.

As she rushed along, Doro caught sight of a male figure emerging from a cross-path and came to a dead stop. Tension filled her until she recognized him as one of her students. "Brian Miller, you startled me."

"Sorry, Professor Banyon. I didn't expect to see anyone out so early on a Saturday morning," the young man blurted out. "That is, not many folks get up at dawn on the weekend." He shifted from one foot to the other. "I better get going."

"What are you doing out at this hour?" Although students were free to leave their dormitories as early as five in the morning, he was right about few doing so on a weekend.

"I—uh—that is, I had to run an errand," he muttered almost under his breath.

"What sort of errand?" she asked.

Brian swallowed convulsively. "You know I'm a pledge, and we do tasks for the brothers. I was just doing one."

The excuse was too vague. "This is the prelude to prank week. You weren't involved in any overnight mischief, were you?"

"No. I wouldn't do anything after curfew, Professor Banyon. I know that's a violation of the rules, and I respect them."

The quick reply did not convince Doro, but she had no grounds to further question the boy. General observations would be better. "You're one of my best students, and you've indicated an interest in taking my new mystery writing class next year. I'd hate to see you lose the privilege by getting involved in foolish antics with your fraternity."

His narrow shoulders slumped. "I'll remember."

"I hope so," Doro said in a stern tone. And she hoped he had not already done something irreparably imprudent. "You realize President Adams has warned the fraternity presidents about stealing valuable items."

"I do. We heard all about the sterling silver baseball trophies that got filched way-back-when and the old statue being dug up."

"It was a statue of the college's most winning baseball coach. His family donated it after he died on the Titanic. Very disrespectful."

Brian hung his head. "Yes, Professor Banyon. If you'll excuse me..." As soon as the words were out of his mouth, he dashed off.

She stared after him. Such strange behavior. After a moment, Doro continued on until she reached Main Street. The bakery and the constable's office were the only places with light pouring from their windows. Were Ev and Wade both present? Or were they out searching for clues—and for suspects? She reached for the doorknob, which easily turned, so at least one of them was around. As soon as Doro stepped inside, she saw the two lawmen behind the counter. Both, their eyes red-rimmed and heavily-shadowed, looked up.

Surprise lit Ev's gaze. "What are you doing here? It's barely dawn."

"I know." Doro lifted the bag she had been carrying. "I thought you could use coffee and a snack, so I went to College Hall, where President Adams explained what happened."

With one hand, Ev rubbed his whisker-covered cheeks. "He was beside himself when I last saw him."

Wade, looking as scruffy as Ev, nodded. "I can't blame him. That manuscript is nearly priceless. The Smiths won't be happy about it being stolen."

"I only met them last night, so I don't know how they'll react," Doro said.

Wade snorted. "Rich people expect everything to go their way. Like your friend Ingram. He thinks he can sweep in and resume his relationship with Aggie."

The comment surprised Doro. Why was Wade still fretting over Rud and Aggie? "They didn't have a real relationship, and Aggie doesn't want anything to do with him. She told you that."

As the constable's head fell forward, he rubbed his neck. "I know. I'm a jealous old fool."

Ev clasped his friend's shoulder. "You're a fool for being jealous, but you aren't old."

The grimness left Wade's face. "Thanks, buddy."

"If your best friend can't tell you the truth, who will?" Ev stepped back as he spoke.

"My best girl told me, and I should've listened better." Wade's attention went to Doro. "I'll tell her I lost my composure, so you won't have to. Ingram bothers me, and it's mostly a personal thing. Not much to do with being a lawman."

She put both hands up. "I wasn't planning to tell." When Wade looked askance, Doro smiled. "I figured you'd own up to it."

Color suffused his broad face. "Thanks."

"I have some doubts about Ingram, too, and it's not personal," Ev put in.

"Did Aggie tell you about what I overheard between him and the Devlins?" Doro asked Wade.

He nodded. "I'm not sure what to make of it. Aggie said Ingram admitted to owing the Devlins a lot of money."

"He did," Doro agreed. "He can't pay until his house is sold, which could be a while. Hank and Cereta sounded desperate."

"Which makes him a suspect in the theft," Wade said. "Especially since he sold the Stutz Bearcat and used the money for other debts."

"That looks bad for Rud, but I'm not sure about Hank, either," Doro murmured.

"We've got plenty to consider." Ev glanced at Doro's bag. "Some refreshments sound good to me. Why don't we sit down? Then, we can tell you what little we know."

The group settled at the battered round table situated near a woodstove. In winter, it provided warmth. Now, it was simply a good place to gather. After pouring coffee and laying out cookies, Doro waited expectantly.

"This is great," Wade observed after a cookie and several swallows of the fragrant brew. "I ran home to change but didn't bother with a shave or a snack."

"You're a lifesaver," Ev said between bites.

Repressing a grin was impossible. "I'm glad I brought enough for four."

Ev's forehead. "Four? There are only three of us."

"I'm not eating," she replied, "but both of you eat enough sweets for two people."

"Very funny," Ev murmured before consuming another cookie.

"I thought so," she said.

"I do, too," Wade chimed in.

Finally, Ev chuckled along with them. "It was mildly amusing. Now, if you want to know about the case, such as it is, we should talk."

All traces of humor left Doro. "President Adams mentioned seeing Hank Devlin."

Wade slumped back in his chair. "Yep, he did but Devlin didn't appear to have anything under his light jacket. Adams didn't ask since he thinks the guy is as honest as the day is long."

Disappointment assailed Doro. "I see."

A rueful smile touched Ev's mouth. "It's not impossible that Devlin tucked the book away or even hid it somewhere."

"We won't rule him out," the constable added.

"What about the group President Adams saw? Any idea who was in it?" Doro asked.

"No, we don't even know if they were students or visitors, although they were likely pledges or other kids out past curfew,"

Ev replied. "We may learn more as the day progresses. Last year, we got complaints about noisy students in the streets ahead of and during prank week."

"That's happened every year I've been constable," Wade put in. "I remember similar noise issues from when I was growing up, too."

"So, do I," Doro agreed, "but President Adams has tried to rein the boys in."

"He's done a good job," Wade observed. "What worries me is the competition among the pledge classes. They always want to outdo one another, and snagging the manuscript would be a coup, so we can't rule it out."

"There are others who might've set their sights on it, as well," Ev said. "For me, Devlin and Ingram are top suspects, along with the pledges."

Both men stated genuine possibilities. "We know applications for the freshmen class in the fall are way down, and I've heard from some of my students that they may not be back. Aggie says the same," Doro said.

Ev released a long breath. "Which means fraternities could nab the book and try to sell it in order to keep some of the brothers in school."

"It's a long shot, but an idea," Wade added.

"Whoever stole it had to be watching for when you left." Doro glanced at Wade. "Could the fire at the Little place have been set to distract you? Maybe someone thought both of you would go."

Wade scratched his head. "Not likely. One of the kids fed the critters late. He had a lantern, which he forgot about. A donkey kicked it over and the hay caught fire immediately. Luckily, all the animals got out, and no one was hurt. The barn's a loss, though."

"I'm sorry about the barn, but the rest is good news." While Wade's explanation seemed valid, Doro did not completely dismiss the idea that a person, not an animal, broke the lantern. "Did you learn anything else? I know the middle of the night isn't an ideal time to investigate."

"We split up to look for the group of guys before meeting back here," Ev replied. "Then, we went to the bakery, because they were working. It was just Stu Adler, the owner, and Micah Burns, his assistant. Stu heard male voices and laughter about the time President Adams noted seeing the group. Micah mentioned seeing two people, maybe a man and a woman. Maybe a man and a boy. He said one voice was deep and the other was softer, but he couldn't understand what they were saying."

Doro bit her lip. "A young couple could've been out. For students, it would be past curfew, and most townsfolk expect their young ones to be home well before midnight, too. Not that some sweethearts don't break the rules."

"That's been the case forever," Wade agreed, "and, sometimes even older couples take a late walk."

The constable's cryptic tone drew Doro's attention. Before she could reply, Ev spoke up.

"Were you among the young ones who broke rules, Constable?" Amusement glittered in his silver gaze.

Color rushed into Wade's face. "Of course not, but we're not talking about me." He cleared his throat. "We need to focus on who was out last night."

After exchanging an amused glance with Ev, Doro addressed the matter at hand. "The Adlers live close to campus, so that makes sense. His daughter Bonnie works the front counter when the shop opens."

"Stu told us that his daughter and wife sleep later due to that fact," Wade put in. "It's doubtful Bonnie saw anyone, but one of us will go back to the bakery later and ask her."

"We should speak with Ingram, too," Ev said."

"We're lucky the presentation is scheduled for tomorrow afternoon," Wade murmured. "We have time to recover the book."

A snippet of conversation from the previous evening returned to Doro. "When I spoke with the Smiths before dinner, we discussed the book. Vance made an off-hand comment about knowing an antiquities dealer and not understanding why old stuff, like the book, is valuable."

"I don't understand it myself," Wade said.

"Rare items are valuable, and that book is one of a kind," Ev put in. "But the comment puts young Smith in a bad light. Would he steal a manuscript his family is donating?"

For a long moment, silence fell over the group. "Hank, Rud, and Vance were in the same fraternity, and Hank was Rud's little brother," Doro observed.

"Interesting, but where are you going with those facts?" Wade inquired.

A slight smile touched Doro's lips. "Maybe they concocted a scheme to get the money Rud owes Hank."

Wade stroked his chin. "And a whole lot more if they sell that book."

"That's for sure," Ev put in.

The telephone ringing interrupted. Wade crossed to the counter and answered. He returned to the table after a quick conversation. "It was President Adams. When he informed the Smiths, who were predictably upset, they immediately offered a reward. A big one."

"How much?" Doro inquired.

"Five-thousand dollars," was Wade's reply.

A low whistle left Ev. "Even split three ways, it would cover Ingram's debt to Adler and Devlin with some left over, which supports collusion."

"I'm not sure about that. According to Adams, the son was there, and he tried to talk his folks out of putting up money. He argued that it's a pledge prank. Only after the mother burst into tears did young Smith agree. Even then, he thought the amount was too much," Wade said.

Doro let her head fall back while she considered the revelations. "I suppose word is going out this morning about the reward."

"Yep, I promised to help spread it," Wade replied. "Mr. Smith also thinks it's a fraternity prank. Because he doesn't want the boys to get in trouble, he asked his son to be the go-between."

"And the kid was happy to do it," Ev suggested.

Wade shook his head. "Adams said his mother had to cajole him again. Young Smith wasn't sure about the frat boys taking it and worried about having to deal with real crooks. Finally, they all agreed that word could go out about contacting him. Then, he'll pick the book up in a public place, get it to his parents, and keep mum about who has it. Adams wasn't as enthusiastic about the plan, but he wants the book back by Sunday afternoon. The husband insisted no charges be filed, and his wife agreed. They got a lot of press attention after an attempted break-in at their home a while back. They don't want more."

"In wealthy circles, people only want to be on the society pages," Doro commented. "Or so my Gramma Rose has said. She's not in that class, but she knew some folks who were."

"Then, their stance makes sense," Ev said.

"Getting the book is most important. If it's a fraternity prank, not charging students is a kindness." Doro relayed her meeting with Brian Miller on her way to town before adding her perspective. "He's a good student, but last fall, he was excited about pledging his father's old fraternity. While Brian would never steal something on his own, I don't think he was doing an errand for one of the brothers at dawn. When I mentioned past pranks, he knew all about them."

"Interesting," Ev added. "He could've been involved in another lark."

"Foolish kids with too much time on their hands," Wade muttered.

"Maybe so, but I'm suspicious of them being involved," Doro agreed.

"President Adams plans to talk to the fraternity presidents this morning," Ev said. "I need to be there with him. His plan is to meet at eight-thirty."

Wade glanced at his watch. "It's just before six o'clock. I'll talk with Dr. Devlin."

Doro shifted toward the constable. "As a witness or as a suspect?" She did not want to believe Hank would steal, but the possibility loomed large.

Wade grimaced. "He doesn't need to know he's a suspect, so I'll be careful with my questions."

"While you're doing that, I want to take our fingerprinting kit and see if I can get any decent ones off the lavatory window or the showcase," Ev said. "I'll bring whatever I get back here."

"I'll have to chat with Mrs. Devlin, too, to see if she can confirm her husband's story," Wade said, "and I can talk with the hotel owners and staff. It's unlikely any of them were out, but you never know."

An opportunity to work more directly in the case came to Doro. "Bonnie Adler will be getting ready for work soon. I could stop by the house under the guise of finalizing our dessert order for tonight's dance. Mrs. Jones handled most of that, but it wouldn't be odd for the chairwoman to inquire."

Ev's dark brows rose. "Wouldn't it be strange for her to go to the house, not the bakery?"

"Not necessarily. This is a small town, and I've known Bonnie since we were children. She was behind me in school, but her sister Inez was in my class. Although we weren't close, we were friendly," Doro replied. "Besides, Mrs. Jones worked with Bonnie, not her father, on the order."

Ev turned his attention to Wade. "What do you think? I don't want Doro putting herself in jeopardy."

The last statement surprised Doro. "How would I be in jeopardy by visiting neighbors I've known for years?'

His gray gaze met hers. "The Adlers need money. Bonnie must know that. What if she and her dad joined forces to steal the book?"

For several seconds, Doro mulled over the completely new prospect. At first blush, it seemed ludicrous. After more consideration, she realized it was possible, although not probable. "I don't want to think they were involved, but I'll say I hope hijinks from the pledges being out didn't disturb her mother and mention our order for tonight. That's not too snoopy."

A grin slowly spread across Ev's face. "You would make a good copper."

Wade chuckled. "She would."

Pleasure spread through Doro. "I'll go by the Adler house on my way back to campus."

Ev met Doro's gaze. "After you speak with Bonnie, maybe you and Aggie could walk around campus and see if there's any talk about fraternity pranks or the missing book."

"That's a good idea. We're sure to run into students, alumni, and faculty. Some of the graduation classes are having individual meetings. Later, sports team members are gathering. The alumni will take on students in a baseball game this afternoon at one-thirty. We might get information then. Or beforehand, since I've heard the alumni team is practicing around eleven o'clock."

"I'd like to go with you to the practice," Ev said to Doro.

"Sounds fine," Wade put in. "I want that manuscript back as soon as possible, but at least by Sunday brunch."

"If Hank, Rud, and Vance are working together, that seems likely. The same with the fraternity boys. I'm sure they'd jump at a big windfall," Doro observed.

"Are you leaning in one direction or the other?" Wade asked.

"Not yet," Doro replied. "What about you, Ev?"

He slumped back in his chair and crossed his arms over his lean waist. "Last night, it sounded like young Smith and Ingram spend time together in the city. Most likely in speakeasies."

"What did they say?" Wade asked.

Doro recapped the conversation and added Mr. Smith's observations about his son. "To me, *glad rags* and painting the *town red* mean going to speakeasies."

"Agree," Wade muttered.

"On our way out last night, Ev and I saw Rud and Vance together, they were talking quietly," Doro said.

"The big reward reveals the Smiths didn't lose a lot of money in the crash, but what about their son and Ingram?" Wade asked.

"Rud owed money to Hank Devlin before the crash. Maybe he owed others, like gangsters, since he sold the Stutz Beartcat recently instead of long ago like he made it sound."

For a moment, silence echoed in the room. Finally, Wade broke it. "We've got a lot to do."

With a sigh, Ev stood up. "We do, but we have help." He winked at Doro. "I'll walk you partway to the Adler house. I want to get rid of this stubble before going to Adams' office."

Although accustomed to seeing Ev clean-shaven, Doro didn't mind the dark shadow covering his jaw. It was the smoky smudges beneath his red-rimmed eyes that bothered her. He needed sleep, but she withheld the observation and focused on matters at hand. "Not many people would've been out when the manuscript was stolen. Mr. Adler would probably be getting up at that time, since he begins baking in the middle of the night. Him hearing voices supports that. I'll see if I can get the exact time he leaves from Bonnie and find out if she heard anyone."

"All right," Ev said.

Doro stood up and addressed Wade. "Aggie and I will meet with the two of you later."

"By then, we'll all have additional information," the constable said. "We can pool it and decide how to proceed."

A worried expression blanketed Ev's face as he looked at Doro. "Have you seen Mr. Adler much since we talked to him during the Frotis case?"

"A couple of times, including yesterday. Why?"

Tension radiated from Ev in waves. "I doubt if he took the manuscript, but it's possible. Remembering how mad he was yesterday and during the Frotis case. I don't know. Just be cautious."

"Always," she promised. "See you later, Wade."

Ev also addressed the constable. "I'll be back after the meeting in Adams' office."

"I should be back myself. See you then."

After she and Ev were on the sidewalk, Doro turned to him as they walked along. "Our best hope is that someone saw pledges around College Hall about the time Wade was called away."

"That'd make the investigation easier, but it isn't the only prospect."

"No, it isn't." For several moments, they continued down the quiet street. Although Doro remained silent, she considered an issue lingering in the back of her mind. "Wade seems sure the fire at the Little place wasn't set to distract him and you. What are your thoughts?"

With one hand, Ev rubbed his neck. "The story is one of the kids left a lantern in the barn, and it got kicked over. Probably by the donkey. Mortimer Little wouldn't have purposefully set a fire, and it's unlikely anyone in his family would."

For a moment, Doro considered the ages of his offspring. "His kids are all under thirteen, so that rings true. It just seems so coincidental, and I don't like coincidences, especially when a crime is involved."

A half-smile moved his lips. "That's because you're an avid mystery reader and an author. Happenstance doesn't work well in fiction, but it occurs in real life."

Doro shoved her hands into her pockets. "It hasn't played a role in any of our previous cases. Did you ever experience it in other investigations?"

Ev shook his head. "Not to any great degree. However, it is possible, and I honestly don't think the fire was set on purpose, although I won't dismiss the idea."

"All right. It just seems strange. Wade always goes to fires with the volunteer firemen. His dad was one of the first volunteers in Michaw, and Wade has always pitched in when he was home from the railroad and since he took over as constable."

"Which is something everyone in town knows," Ev added.

"It is, but I'm not sure how many students would be aware of his background."

"Very few is my guess."

When they reached the turnoff to the Adler place, the couple paused. "Maybe it's wishful thinking, but I can't shake the idea that taking the book was a fraternity prank. I just can't figure how they would know the showcase would be unguarded for a time," Doro said.

"Maybe they didn't. Maybe they were out looking for an opportunity to pull a big prank and happened to see Wade leave. After all, College Hall has been a target for antics in the past, hasn't it?"

"It has, but we're pursuing all avenues. By later today, we may have this case solved." Doro hoped so. Another study of Ev's fatigue-lined face revealed he had pushed beyond his limits, and Wade had, too. While she felt stressed, Doro had gotten a good night's sleep. But, if the book was not found, it might be her last one for a while.

Chapter Eight

After leaving Ev near the campus, Doro headed toward the Adler home. Bonnie should be up but her ailing mother might not be, so Doro tapped on the front door. Within moments, the young woman, clad in a wrapper, answered. Evidently, Bonnie had not been up long because her stylish and crimped bob was disheveled.

"Doro, what a surprise."

Although Bonnie's tone and expression did not exude welcome, Doro smiled. "It's nice to see you again. I haven't been in the bakery since you returned."

Several moments of silence passed before the other young woman responded. "I need to get ready for work. Do you want something?"

Doro maintained her pleasant demeanor. "Just a few minutes of your time." Bonnie slowly opened the door, but only a little, which meant Doro had to squeeze inside. "Maybe we could sit down."

A harsh breath left Bonnie. "All right, but I don't have much time." She pivoted on her heel and strode down the hallway to the back of the house.

As Doro followed in her wake, she wondered if Bonnie would answer questions. When they entered the expansive kitchen, the aroma of coffee melded with the scent of cinnamon. Doro inhaled deeply. "What wonderful smells. Do you bake at home, too?"

Bonnie's expression softened. "I love baking, but Pa won't let me do any in the bakery. When I came home, I wanted to help…" Her voice trailed off before she again gained steam. "He only wants a counter girl."

"He may change his mind."

After pouring two cups of coffee, Bonnie gestured to the table. "Sit down and help yourself to a roll." She pushed a notepad to one side. "I have to make a list for our neighbor, who comes to check on Ma during the day. The woman can't read Pa's writing, which is mostly print instead of longhand, but he only went through sixth grade."

The criticism in the girl's voice bothered Doro. "Your father has worked since then, from what I know." Stuart Adler had not had an easy life. Didn't his daughter appreciate his sacrifices?

"Yeah, he had to quit school to help his family," Bonnie conceded. After sitting down, she made two more notations on the paper. "He could write better, though."

As the girl spoke and wrote, Doro noted Bonnie's flowing script. "Your handwriting is lovely."

Bonnie beamed at her. "I won penmanship awards every year in school. I was really good at the drills and such."

"How nice." Although Doro's own handwriting was fine, she considered the focus on penmanship instruction to be largely a waste of time. Literature, history, and civics were far more intriguing.

Bonnie pointed to the small pitcher of cream and the sugar bowl next to it. "Help yourself."

"Thank you." Doro lightened her coffee and put one of the cinnamon buns on the plate provided by Bonnie. After enjoying some of both, Doro smiled. "Delicious."

Bonnie took a chair. "I'm glad you like it."

"I love the rolls. You're very talented. Has your father tasted these?"

"No, he eats his sweets at work, but Ma loves them."

"I understand why." After more coffee and another bite of roll, Doro got down to business. "I don't want to hold you up, so I'll get to the point of why I came. You may have heard about the valuable manuscript that's being given to the college this weekend."

"Everyone's heard about it," Bonnie said. "It's hard to believe a book could cause such a stir. Not that I don't love to read, because I do."

"This particular book is nearly one of a kind." When the other woman made no response, Doro continued. "Anyhow, it was stolen last night, so we're trying to find out if anyone saw or heard something odd around two-thirty this morning."

"I'm not up then." Bonnie lifted her cup to her lips and took several swallows.

Was the calm reaction a result of already knowing about the theft or of not caring? Either seemed possible. "Most folks aren't, but I wondered if you heard noises. There were reports of loud voices not far from here. I know pain sometimes keeps your mother from sleeping. Maybe she heard something."

Bonnie's brow furrowed. "Ma took the strong medicine last night, so she wouldn't have been up. Now that I think about it, and I don't know what time it was, I heard laughter and voices at some point. I like to keep my window open a crack when the weather isn't bitter cold."

"I see." When Bonnie still did not look up, Doro finished her coffee and roll before pushing the plate and cup aside. "Did you look out your window to see who was causing a ruckus?"

The question brought Bonnie's head up. "It wasn't a ruckus, just some students having fun. That's not unusual. Since we live close to the campus, I've heard them all my life." A wistful expression blanketed her face. "I wanted to go to college so bad, and Ma thought we could afford it. That was before Sam went off to war and came back sick. He couldn't work and needed lots of doctoring. The bills and the trips to soldier hospitals took a lot of money. Now, Ma is sick, so I gotta help Pa with the bakery because he can't afford extra workers. Otherwise, I'd still be in the city."

"You lived with Inez, didn't you?"

"For a while," Bonnie replied. "Late last year, I got an apartment with some other girls. A real nice one. Now, I'm stuck here, and money is tight."

Her admission reminded Doro of Rud's confrontation with Mr. Adler. "Were you working yesterday when your father got into an argument in front of the shop?"

Color rushed into the girl's face. "Pa shouldn't have argued like he did, but he goes off sometimes. Ma says he's not himself cuz of all that's happened to our family. He's not the same, for sure."

"In what way?"

Bonnie ran one forefinger around the rim of her cup. "His temper and his forgetfulness."

The latter piqued Doro's interest. "Your father's memory is failing?" She knew about him mixing up orders, but was more involved?

"Ma says it's all from stress, that he gets tired and confused. Maybe so. I just know I had to come home and help because she can't do it anymore."

"Your father had a right to be upset if he didn't get paid for Sam's car." Doro was careful to avoid a direct question.

"Rud says he gave Pa all the money long ago," Bonnie insisted. "He wouldn't lie."

Bonnie's use of Rud's nickname sent a jolt of surprise through Doro. "Did you talk to Rud recently?"

The younger woman's gaze went to the table. "He loves sweets, and I worked in the bakery after school when he was in college. He came in two or three times a week. He's real nice, not like Pa claims."

"You knew about him buying Sam's vehicle years ago." Doro made it a statement.

Bonnie gnawed on her lower lip. "Sure. Sam hated to sell it, but he could hardly get out of the house, let alone drive. Rud says he paid, and I believe him."

"You discussed it since the confrontation between him and your father?"

Bonnie kept her attention away from Doro. "I knew when he bought the automobile. I told Rud how hard it was for Sam and Pa to sell it, but we needed money. Rud understood." Bonnie got to her feet. "Sorry. I gotta finish getting ready for work. Pa will be mad if I'm late."

Before she had to leave, Doro needed more information. "You said your father leaves much earlier than you. About what time would that be?"

Bonnie hesitated before responding. "He's usually gone by three-thirty, but I don't see or hear him as a rule because I'm a sound sleeper."

"But the voices outside woke you?"

A flush put color in Bonnie's ivory complexion. "I woke to use the lavatory. Now, I really have to get going."

"Of course. You'll have a long day, what with bringing sweets to the dance."

The girl's expression brightened. "It will be fun. I love music, and I get to wear a pretty dress instead of the drab outfits Pa expects me to wear in the bakery. Besides, we'll leave the treats and trays to pick up tomorrow, so we won't stay too late."

"That's good," Although Doro wanted to ask more questions, time had run out. "Thanks for sharing your breakfast. If you recall more about what you heard early this morning, please let me know."

"Sure. I'll show you out."

With no alternative, Doro let Bonnie escort her to the front door. Once outside, Doro went to Wheaton Hall, where she found Aggie waiting for her. "Let's go to my place and talk." Getting her friend's perspective would be useful.

Aggie frowned. "Is something wrong? I got your note about taking coffee and cookies to Ev, but I figured you'd come right back here."

After glancing around and seeing no one, Doro replied. "Something is wrong, but not with Ev or Wade, and I'd rather discuss it in private."

A moment's hesitation preceded Aggie's response "All right."

After they settled on the divan in Doro's apartment, she caught her friend up on the latest developments. "I'm hoping fraternity boys took it as a prank, since we have a better chance of getting it back quickly in that case."

Aggie leaned back and folded her hands in her lap. "Ev may have news after the meeting with President Adams." She chewed on her lower lip. "But the book is valuable. Many people know that, and they knew where it was."

"That's what makes me uneasy," Doro said. "Ev and Wade feel certain the fire at the Little place was accidental and not a ploy."

"Wade went there, right?"

Doro nodded. "He helped put it out."

Concern shadowed Aggie's hazel gaze. "You said he's fine."

"Hale and hardy, although both he and Ev are exhausted. Not that they admitted to it."

Aggie's expression softened. "Not a surprise. Our men are more progressive than many, especially when it comes to accepting women as their equals, but they don't like to own up to weakness."

A chuckle escaped Doro. "They don't, but getting back to the fire. They're both sure it wasn't set."

"You aren't."

For a moment, Doro stared into the distance and considered the clues. When she looked back at her friend, she shrugged. "It seems too coincidental. We've all discussed not believing in coincidence in the past. Now, Ev alluded to me reading too many mysteries. He says in real life, sometimes happenstance occurs."

"He really said your love of whodunits is affecting your judgment?" Surprise underscored the question. "He always praises your intellect and intuition."

"He wasn't critical or mean." Doro heard the defensive note in her voice.

"Of course not. I'm only surprised he offered even the slightest criticism."

Doro nodded. "So was I, but his point was well-taken. And Ev pointed out that Wade's experience fighting fires means he'd notice if it had been set."

A thoughtful expression blanketed Aggie's face. "That's true, but someone clever and desperate could've made it look like an accident."

"They'll keep the idea in mind. However, I got the impression it's way in the back of their minds. Bonnie Adler hearing male voices and laughter supports the most likely culprits being fraternity pledges, although Hank Devlin being out is troubling. Any of them could've seen an opportunity when Wade left College Hall."

"True, but let's hope it was pledges, and let's hope they own up to the theft right away. Then, another case will be closed."

Aggie's smile did not quite reach her eyes, and when Doro responded in kind, she felt sure hers looked equally weak. "Since our fellas want us to see if there's campus gossip, why don't we walk around? We can do that under the guise of greeting visitors."

"Good guise, since we're on the committee. I'm ready to go if you are."

With that, the pair headed out of Wheaton Hall. The number of people crisscrossing the campus had grown by leaps and bounds during the short time Doro had been in her apartment. Since many were headed to class meetings, they merely offered greetings and moved on. "So far, we're not learning anything," Doro murmured.

"Maybe we should walk by College Hall. Ev will be leaving the meeting in President Adams' office soon. Even though you said we'd come to the constable's office later, we might find out something from him now. Besides, students, faculty, and alumni will be around there."

"Let's head that way," Doro agreed.

As they ambled toward the center of campus, the two friends encountered familiar faces. Two were Hank and Cereta Devlin. Doro stopped. "Hello." Although she offered a smile with the greeting, the couple simply nodded. When the Devlins would have walked on, Doro spoke again. "Have you been to our class meeting, Hank? I was sorry not to make it, but other duties prevailed." Posing a benign question seemed like the best way to begin.

Hank stopped first while his wife took several more steps before casting a scowl in his direction. "I'd like to get back to our room and freshen up before lunch." Her sharp tone could have cut wood.

An exasperated sigh escaped her husband. "We're going in a minute because I want to get to the ball field for practice." He looked back at Doro and Aggie. "I'm playing on the alumni team."

"I thought practice was at eleven," Aggie said.

Hank shrugged. "It is, but a handful of us are going early. I haven't played ball in an age. If you'll excuse us."

"We wouldn't want to hold you up, but I wondered if you heard talk about the missing book." Hank's shoulders went rigid while Cereta's face lost color. Their reactions disturbed Doro, and she anxiously waited for answers.

"Someone mentioned it to us," Hank replied. "I didn't pay much attention."

Because he did not meet her gaze, Doro's suspicions escalated. "It's a major concern."

"It certainly is," Aggie added. "I'm surprised people weren't widely discussing it. Our class meeting in the big lecture hall near the showcase. Surely, most of our classmates had to walk by and see the broken glass front boarded up."

Hank cleared his throat. "They did."

The two-word response seemed like stonewalling, so Doro pressed the point. "You two had to see it."

"Uh-no. I went inside, but I didn't pay much attention to the showcase," Cereta responded.

"Neither did I," her husband agreed. "Now, we really should be on our way."

His wife slipped her hand into the crook of his arm, and the pair hurried off. For a long moment, Doro stared at their retreating figures. "They acted strangely."

Aggie rolled her eyes. "I agree about that."

"The broken showcase should've been a topic of gossip," Doro put in. "Hank and Cereta acted like it was no concern at all."

"We have something to tell Ev and Wade, but let's go on and see if we can learn more."

⁂

An hour later, the two friends headed to the constable's office. Fatigue and frustration tugged at Doro. "There's gossip, but we didn't get much additional information."

"We know most people believe it was a fraternity prank, so it'll be interesting to discover what Ev learned at the meeting," Aggie said.

Her friend's observation lifted Doro's spirits a notch. "Maybe something significant came up. He might even know who took it." That would be the best possible news.

"Maybe so," her friend murmured.

When the pair reached the familiar constable's building, they went inside to find their lawmen beaus in deep conversation at the table. Ev and Wade stood up as their sweethearts approached.

As soon as she saw Ev's expression, Doro felt a stab of dismay. If he had good news about the book, he would not look so grim.

"Sit down." Wade gestured to the two empty chairs on either side of his and Ev's.

"Thank you." Aggie took a seat.

Doro forced a smile when she sat next to Ev. "What did you find out at the meeting?"

"I'd like to know," Aggie put in.

"We all would," Wade said before looking at Ev. "Tell the girls about your meeting."

Ev's grimace deepened. "The fraternity presidents acted like their pledges would never steal something valuable. We all know that's happened in the past."

"The end of the pledge term always creates a few issues," the constable said in a calm, composed voice. "This time, it seems like the chapter presidents are edgier than usual."

"Guilty consciences is my guess," Ev said.

"Did any of the chapter presidents admit that their pledges were out-and-about last night?"

He leaned forward, braced his elbows on his knees, and stared at the empty stove. "They all admitted most pledges were out looking for some big stunt to pull."

"Stealing the book would definitely be an achievement," Aggie put in.

"It would be one of the biggest ever," Doro agreed. "Bigger than when freshmen boys put a banner across the front of College Hall years ago. Bigger than snatching the sterling silver trophies. Bigger than digging up the statue."

Ev drove his fingers through his clipped hair. "I'll never understand college kids and their antics."

"Most students are serious about school," Doro pointed out.

"They were when we were undergraduates, and it's still true," Aggie added.

Ev released a long, low breath. "Both of you were, I'm sure. I didn't mean any criticism. I'm just..." His voice trailed off.

"Exhausted," Doro supplied.

He offered a faint smile. "Tired, but so is Wade."

The constable scratched his head. "I won't deny it."

Aggie laid one hand over his. "We'll find the book. Then, both of you can catch up on your sleep."

"Sounds good to me," her fiancé replied.

"Me, too, but we're not close to solving this case," Ev murmured. "President Adams brought up the reward right away. Evidently, he had the news spread at all the class meetings this morning."

Doro and Aggie exchanged a long look.

"I've seen you two engage in silent communication before," Wade put in. "What's going on?"

The friends grinned before Aggie gestured for Doro to tell the tale. "When we spoke with the Devlins a short time ago, we talked about the book being missing. They were coming from a class meeting, and they didn't act like the book being stolen was of much interest."

"That's odd," Ev said.

Wade nodded "It sure is, especially when they had to hear about the huge reward. What else did they say?"

"Not a lot," Doro replied before reviewing what the Devlins had said and done.

Ev and Wade exchanged a long look. "Interesting," the constable said.

"Very much so," Ev agreed. "I'm inclined to think pledges were involved, but we can't rule Devlin out. I'd like to know why Mrs. Devlin mentioned not going with him last night, and it not turning out well. It sure sounds like he wasn't simply taking a walk."

"He was gone when I went to the hotel early this morning," Wade said. "Now, we'll have to catch him at the ball field."

"I'm planning to go to the practice," Doro put in, "and stay for some of the game."

"I'll go with you," Ev said. "Will that work for you, Wade?"

"Absolutely. Since you're both employed on campus, that makes sense," the constable replied.

Doro grinned. "Wonderful. Rud may be there, too. He played baseball in college."

"I'd like to talk to him, since Bonnie Adler heard noise in the night," Ev said. "We know a little from Wade talking with her father and his assistant already."

The constable nodded. "After I missed Devlin at the hotel, I went by the bakery. Since Stu and my dad were friends, I figured he might be more cooperative with me."

"And he was, I bet" Doro observed.

"Pretty much. I framed the conversation as wanting witnesses. Stu didn't see anyone on his way to work, but Micah, his assistant, heard those people when he passed by the campus around two-thirty."

"Which was about the time you were apprised of the fire," Aggie said.

"That's right," Wade replied.

The information provided a new idea to Doro. "Wade, you've been sure that the fire wasn't set, and you have expertise in that arena. But what if whoever stole the manuscript wasn't involved in the fire, but heard about it and took advantage of you needing to leave College Hall? With all the volunteer firemen going to the Little place, they would've seen by anyone who was out late."

"An excellent point," the constable said.

"It sure is," Ev agreed.

"Doro always makes good points," Aggie added.

Ev grinned at Doro. "She sure does, and this one helps. So does Micah hearing two guys talking. Now, we need to find out who they were. One could've been your student, Doro."

She chewed on her lower lip. "Possibly, because the pledges could've split into groups of two or three, so they're still suspects."

"Agreed," Wade said. "Although Devlin was alone when President Adams saw him, that doesn't mean he didn't meet someone before then."

"So, we have a few top suspects. Devlin, Ingram, and fraternity pledges. Stu Adler can't be one because Micah would've recognized his voice," Ev pointed out.

Briefly, Doro considered the observation. "True, but there's a small chance Stu and Micah worked together. Bonnie says her father isn't himself these days." She revealed the forgetfulness and his temper.

Wade scratched his head. "Stu's had a lot on his mind, but chances of him taking the book are small. I'm willing to put them at the bottom of the suspect list. What about the rest of you?"

Aggie immediately agreed. "That makes sense to me."

Ev followed suit. "Me, too. What about you, Doro?"

"I concur. Despite the Adlers' money problems, I don't see him breaking into College Hall, with or without Micah or Bonnie," she said. "But the changes in him mean he might not remember about being paid."

"You're right," Wade said.

"But we know Ingram owes Devlin," Ev reminded them.

"There's still a chance of them colluding with Vance," Doro added. "Bonnie mentioned hearing people, but shooed me out before I could pin her down."

Aggie sighed. "That's interesting, since she made a point of defending Rud against her father."

"If Mr. Adler is confused, that makes sense," Doro pointed out.

"It does," Aggie agreed. "There's a lot on the table, so what next?"

After bracing his elbows on his knees, Ev leaned forward. "Adams promised the Smiths that charges won't be pressed against the thief, which puts us in a pickle."

Dismay gripped Doro hard. "Are we wasting time pursuing the case?"

"Of course not. We can't be sure the reward will lead to the return of the manuscript, so we've got to keep digging."

Doro slumped in her chair. "Good."

A chuckle left Ev as he reached for her hand. "You can keep on sleuthing."

The warmth of his fingers kept Doro from objecting to the teasing. "Wonderful," she replied.

Ev released his hold and stood up. "You and I were going to the ball field, Doro."

"Hank was on his way when we saw him, so we might catch him before formal practice starts," Doro said. "It's already ten-thirty, maybe we should go to the field now."

Ev winked at her. "Good idea. I'll talk with Adams after that."

"I'll try to get over for a little while, but it depends on what else happens." Wade nodded at his friend and colleague. "Thanks for handling the talk with the frat boys."

Ev nodded. "Wade, I'll see you later at the game."

*

Neither Doro nor Ev spoke again until they were on the sidewalk. "You seemed tentative about the fraternity boys taking the book."

A long, low breath escaped him. "It's a strong possibility, especially in light of your conversation with your student. But it isn't the only one, which we all agreed on. Your talk with the Devlins proves that. Then, there's Ingram. He's in dire need of money."

Doro mentally reviewed the details. "Are you and Wade planning to talk with those two? Neither of you mentioned that." As deep as their discussion was, she realized they had not hit every important point.

"We discussed interviewing them before you and Aggie came in. I mentioned the trio, including young Smith, all belonging to the same fraternity to President Adams earlier."

"What did he say?"

He ground his teeth. "Adams doesn't want Vance Smith questioned, and he'd rather we didn't bother Ingram and Devlin, either. Friendly conversation is all right. Taking them to the office or outright interrogating them is off the table."

"Vance not supporting the reward is a factor against him working with Rud or Hank or both, but I can chat with him."

His expression did not lighten. "Be careful. You don't have tenure yet, and the Smiths could exert pressure if you push their son too hard."

The warning resonated with Doro. If she was going to be the library director, she needed to be a tenured faculty member. Mrs. Smith had already threatened to stop a promotion. Would the woman interfere in the tenure process? For several moments, she considered the risk involved in surging forward with the investigation. "Justice is important."

A grin lit Ev's face. "I'm glad you think so, too." His expression grew solemn. "Remember that we may not be able to file charges, due to President Adams' promise."

"I'd still like to know who took the book and what the plan is," Doro said. "Besides, we can't rule out someone wanting to sell it."

"Good point." He tucked her hand into the crook of his arm.

A pent-up breath escaped Doro. "We've gone over the most likely culprits."

They walked another thirty feet before Ev responded. "I'd add Lester Jonson. I know you like him, but Ingram mentioning larceny had to upset him."

"You and Wade talked about Lester, I assume."

"We did," Ev admitted.

While she did not like that the men had not already shared the idea, Doro offered an excuse for Lester. "That's probably because of the situation with the lost exam."

"Maybe so, but I'll keep an eye on him. He wants to get a master's degree and teach in college, right?"

"Yes."

"Schoolteachers don't make a lot of money. My sister taught before her marriage, so I know the salaries aren't high. Didn't he graduate almost a decade ago?"

"That's right."

"Maybe he's frustrated with having to wait. You're a year younger than him, and you've been a professor for a few years."

The observation evoked a memory of Lester saying how lucky she was to already be living her dream. Doro had not detected jealousy, but how could he not wish to be in her shoes? Although Doro was not sure about Ev's assessment, she reluctantly admitted he might be correct. "All right, but he'd be way down my list."

"Duly noted. According to the roster I saw, he, Devlin, Ingram, and young Smith are all playing in the game this afternoon. I expect to see them there, but we have eyes on Devlin and Ingram. Wade talked to the hotel owner, and he'll call the constable's office and the college if the doctor and his wife check out. Same if Ingram moves from the faculty residence. The front desk knows to send word."

"You and Wade discussed a lot before Aggie and I arrived," Doro pointed out.

"A little."

Doro turned toward Ev. In the past, he had not withheld pertinent details from her—not even during their first case, when she had briefly been a suspect. "Is there anything else I might want to know?" She failed to keep a chill out of her voice.

A harsh breath escaped him. "We didn't intend to keep details from you and Aggie. There's a lot to consider, and we should've gone over every point. Sorry."

Beneath her fingers, Doro felt tension invade Ev. The pressure on him and Wade was immense, which dictated her next words. "Neither of you got much sleep, and I'm sure that took a toll."

"I guess, but we've got to get the book by one o'clock tomorrow. Sleep will come after that."

"Since the alumni group is practicing ahead of the game, we can speak with Rud, Hank, Vance and probably Lester, too. All of them played baseball here. No pointed questions, but I might get a feel for who is involved."

They walked another fifteen feet before Ev responded. "That's a good idea, but almost all your ideas are good."

Pleasure, along with amusement, threaded through Doro. "I won't ask which ones haven't been."

A deep chuckle was his reply.

Within minutes, the pair arrived at the ball diamond, where alumni were already practicing. They stopped near the outfield bleachers to look around.

"Rud and Hank are talking." Ev jerked his head to the right but kept his attention on Doro.

She glanced in that direction. "Since they're standing well away from everyone else, my curiosity is piqued."

A broad smile lit up Ev's face. "You're always sleuthing, so that's no surprise."

Doro rolled her eyes but grinned in return. "Not always."

He shrugged. "But most of the time."

His teasing lifted Doro's spirits no matter what else was on her mind, but she focused on the two men. "Although it's hard to gauge their demeanors from here, neither seemed to be smiling."

"Not a surprise," Ev murmured. "From what you and Aggie said, they're pretty hostile with each other."

"They are now," Doro admitted, "but Rud was Hank's big brother in the fraternity. Usually, that creates a lasting tie, but not with them. Not now."

"One friend owing another lots of money will do that," Ev remarked.

"True," she agreed. "I'd love to know what they're discussing."

"Collusion?"

Doro turned to him. "Quite possibly. I'll need to be circumspect with my questions, but I'll do my best."

Ev's silver gaze warmed. "I know you will."

As always, the connection between them became a palpable force, and Doro had to glance away to refocus on the case. "I don't see Lester." She scanned the area. "He planned to play, and we wanted to speak with him, too."

"I definitely do, but it's still early," Ev replied.

Another male voice intruded and jerked Doro around. Vance Smith was striding toward them, a grin on his face.

"Hey, Doro, you coming for the game?" Vance stopped next to her.

A couple of moments passed before she adjusted to his sudden presence. "Maybe part of it. I have a few other things to do."

"Stay long enough to cheer us old guys on, at least." Vance gestured at his attire. "We saved our uniforms."

"How nice," Ev muttered.

Vance cast a glance at him. "Yep. You know how it is. The artifacts hold more meaning as the years go by. You must've kept some of your old uniforms."

A stony expression froze Ev's features. "No, I didn't keep my old copper uniforms."

Vance's gaze ran over Ev. "You like having a job with a uniform, huh?"

"I like having a job that puts food on the table," Ev bit out.

The other man's jaw tightened. Before Vance could respond, Doro cut in. "From what you said last night before the dinner, you're not much for old things."

After a moment, Vance plucked at his shirt. "This brings back good memories of fun with friends and simpler times."

Doro glanced to where Rud and Hank were still talking. She gestured in their direction. "I'm glad to see the two of them together. They had some tough words yesterday."

A grimace twisted Vance's features. "I asked them to work their situation out."

"You know Rud owes money to Hank?" Doro asked.

"We're old fraternity brothers, so Hank told me about the issue," Vance replied. "It's not such a great sum."

The comment reminded Doro that Vance's family was wealthy, because five-hundred dollars was a lot to the average person.

Ev crossed his arms across his chest. "Since you don't have a wife and children, you may not understand Devlin's dilemma."

Vance's frown deepened. "I wasn't aware you have a family, Officer Mallow. Does your wife know you're escorting Doro to events?"

Color rose like a floodtide in Ev's lean cheeks. "I'm not married, Smith, but I know about taking care of a family, since I did that after my father died." He paused for a heartbeat. "Maybe Ingram and Devlin could join forces and search for the missing book. Your parents' reward would solve the problem between them."

Doro fought back a smile. While Ev was not going against President Adams' wishes by questioning Vance, he was dangling bait. Would Vance take it? So far, he had been circumspect. She put one hand behind her back and crossed her fingers.

Vance's expression did not change. "I don't like them offering so much money, or any at all, but they insisted. I just hope the book comes back before they up the ante. It would be a nice bonus for anyone, including a fraternity. Were you in one, officer?"

"Nope," Ev replied. "I didn't go to college."

"I see. Then, you may not be aware that pledge classes engage in their fair share of hijinks, especially right before going active. At least, that's true here at Michaw College and has been for years." Vance spoke in a lecturing tone.

"Ev has been the campus security officer for over a year-and-a-half, so he is aware of prank week." While she wanted to chastise Vance more, Doro stopped.

A wink from Ev told Doro that he appreciated the support. "I am aware. Last year, nothing major happened, and it's my understanding pledges have pulled back from big stunts."

"They have," Doro agreed.

"Sort of disappointing to a former frat guy," Vance observed.

"So, you don't mind your mother being upset over the book being stolen?" Ev asked.

A hard breath left Vance. "My mother is high-strung. Dad and I told her not to worry. The reward will ensure it comes back, not that it wouldn't have turned up anyhow."

"I hope it does," Doro said. "But there's a chance someone took it to sell to an antiquities dealer. You mentioned knowing one."

Red stained Vance's face. "If you're thinking I took that book…"

Doro cut him off. "Of course not. I was only saying someone taking it to sell was a possibility. Don't you agree?" She kept her tone amiable.

"Possible, but not probable," Vance replied. "Now, I gotta practice."

Before Doro or Ev could say more, he dashed to the other side of the field. When he reached Rud and Hank, both turned to Vance. "I'd love to know what they're saying," Doro murmured.

"You and me both," Ev put in.

As she turned toward him, Doro smiled. "You drew Vance out with your comments, no questions."

His silver gaze sparkled. "He only nibbled on the bait instead of really going for it.

Doro glanced back to where the trio had stood. "They're practicing now, so I'll wait until they come off the field. Then, I'll talk to Hank and Rud. Separately, if possible."

"Sounds good," Ev remarked before looking around. "I don't see Jonson."

Uneasiness crept through Doro. Although she had not considered Lester a strong suspect, Doro wondered if Ev was right to be wary. "He'd need a ride to Sylvania to catch the train."

Ev rubbed his eyes. "I'll head back to Maple Hall and see if he's there. If not, I'll have to go back to the office and find out if he's someplace in town. He may be down the list, but he's on it."

"All right," Doro agreed. "Should we meet up before the dance tonight?"

For a moment, he searched her face. "Take some time to relax. I'll pick you up early unless we get big news. If that happens, I'll call Wheaton Hall."

"I hope you do," Doro said. "For now, I'll sit in the bleachers and watch practice."

"If I can get back before the game, I'll look for you."

After he turned away, Doro called to him. "Ev…"

He glanced over his shoulder. "What?"

"Be careful."

A grin tugged at one corner of his mouth. "I'm just looking for Jonson. Nothing dangerous in that."

"Of course not." Even so, as Doro watched Ev leave the athletic field, she could not dispel the cloud floating through her mind. Being a lawman held hazards, even in the best of times. And this time was not good.

Chapter Nine

Several hours later, Ev escorted Doro into the auditorium for the dance. She had no chance to speak with Rud or Hank at the ball field, since they hurried off after practice. Although Doro had rushed to follow, she could not catch up. The two of them and some others, including Vance, disappeared into their old fraternity house. Since she did not want to hang around for over an hour waiting for the game to start, Doro had gone home.

After Ev came to escort her across campus, she told him about her failure to speak with Rud and Hank. "They were way ahead of me, and I wouldn't have been welcome at the frat house."

"It's interesting they went there, especially together."

"There was a bigger group, but it is a possible clue. Despite Vance being against the reward, he could be negotiating the return of the book. Whether from Rud, Hank, or the fraternity, I can't say."

"I hope he does. As much as I want to know who took it, getting the book back is of utmost importance."

"Did you find Lester?" Doro asked. "When I didn't hear from you, I figured there was no headway with any of this mess."

"We discovered he hasn't left town," Ev said. "I tried calling Wheaton Hall, but no one answered, so I couldn't even leave a message for you. It turns out he injured his right wrist. Doc Silven treated him and said playing ball this afternoon was out. I talked to Doc myself. He gave Jonson something for the pain and suggested he rest until tonight. When I went by Maple Hall, I found out he was sleeping."

"Was it a sprain?"

"That's the interesting part. Doc characterized it as a strain with some scrapes."

The revelations provided more food for thought. "Scrapes like someone could've gotten crawling through the bathroom window in College Hall."

"Exactly. I specifically asked Doc if the abrasion might've been caused by the iron window frame. He wouldn't rule it out."

"I hope Lester didn't take the book," Doro murmured.

Ev slid one arm around her shoulders. "We've already discussed his motive."

"We did, and I didn't agree with you then."

"What about now?" When he released his hold on her, Ev clasped her hand.

"He's moved from way down my list to nearer the top," Doro admitted.

His fingers entwined with hers. "It's crowded up there. Wade and I may have to talk with the Devlins, Jonson, Ingram, and young Smith later. Casually, of course. No interrogations."

"I've mulled over ideas. Maybe the fraternity brothers want to make a dramatic showing by putting it back early tomorrow morning. That's happened with less valuable items in the past. Several years ago, one fraternity stole the signs of all the others. President Adams was furious, but a search of the only house still having its sign proved fruitless. After he threatened to ban that fraternity, the signs showed up on the baseball field one morning before a big game that afternoon."

A snort left Ev. "I don't understand the penchant for pranks, and I never will. They're a waste of time and energy."

Doro clutched his arm as they ambled along. "I agree. Childish pursuits, but it happens every year. In any case, if the book appears tomorrow, I'll be happy."

Several seconds of silence preceded his reply. "So, will I. According to President Adams, the elder Smith seems to think such stunts are amusing."

"From what Vance said earlier, he also does. He was engaged in more than one practical joke while he was a student here."

Ev's expression did not lighten. "Not surprising. I suppose Ingram was, too."

"A few pranks," Doro agreed before turning the conversation to something else of concern. "Hank wasn't involved in as many. Other than taking the exam, Lester never did anything out of line."

As they approached the auditorium, Ev's steps slowed. "So, if Jonson took the book, he didn't work with the other three."

"No, he wouldn't have. If there's complicity, it's only among Rud, Hank, and Vance, with their old fraternity in the mix," Doro observed. "Or just Rud and Vance. Any plot would have to hinge on the big reward. What confuses me is Vance being against the reward."

"Me, too. That's why we still need to consider the pledges and Jonson."

"I can't disagree," Doro murmured. "Usually, we talk about motive, means, and opportunity. In this case, every suspect has all three."

"Which makes it more complicated."

When they reached the doors of the auditorium, he paused to study Doro. "I should have said so already, but you look especially lovely this evening."

She glanced down at the drop-waist sea blue silk dress with its full skirt and elbow-length sleeves. "Thank you." Any compliment from him pleased her enough to push the case out of her mind, at least briefly. "It's new, especially for tonight."

His attention went from the frock back to her face. "It's almost the same color as your eyes. I've never seen the ocean in person, only in pictures, but I bet the water isn't a prettier shade of blue."

Heat flooded her face while pleasure swelled her heart. "Thank you. By the way, you look good yourself." She fingered the sleeve of his navy suit.

"Thank you. I can't let my girl down. You always look pretty, but I loved the ensemble you wore to the speakeasy last summer." A lilt of laughter was in his deep voice.

Doro could not repress a grin. "That's hardly appropriate for a college event."

"Maybe not, but it was eye-catching."

Since that frock was sleeveless and short, it had garnered attention—mostly from Ev. "I still have it, not that I'm planning another speakeasy foray."

"Good, because I'm not, either."

Although she had not felt tense, Doro's muscles slackened. "That's a relief because you'd only be going as part of your job."

He patted the hand resting on his arm. "Being a Prohibition agent is my former job. Working with the Bureau last summer was temporary and one-time. I won't do it again."

The assertions should have relieved her, but a niggling finger of doubt traced her spine. If necessary, Ev would go back to the Bureau. She knew that because she knew him. Duty and dedication were hallmarks of his personality. Even so, Doro managed a casual countenance. "I'm glad."

When they entered the auditorium building, Ev and Doro went right to the big room housing the dance. Only a handful of people were present, but they were early.

"It looks great," Ev said as they stepped inside. "The workers did a good job moving the tables and your committee brought more flowers."

"We only need a few tables for people to sit when not dancing, and the bouquets were freshened. Mrs. Jones oversaw putting lights on the porch, too. The committee debated it. Some folks thought it would look too much like Christmas, but I think they lend a festive touch."

He glanced toward the far end of the room where French doors opened to the outside. "Very pretty, and I see there are a few shrouded corners."

Heat rushed into Doro's cheeks as his observation brought back memories of a town Christmas party held only a few weeks after he had arrived in Michaw. The two of them slipped outside where mistletoe and lights had adorned the porch. "Students are invited to the dance, and a few will likely go outside for fresh air."

"Too bad there's no mistletoe," he whispered.

A glance at Ev revealed laughter in his silver gaze. Doro could not repress a smile. "It is a shame."

"What's a shame?" Aggie's voice broke into the conversation.

Doro turned to see her friend and the town constable. "Nothing. We were just chatting."

Her friend looked from Doro to Ev and back. "All right."

The two words, along with Aggie's expression, telegraphed doubt but Doro moved on. "The fresh flowers make the bouquets look new, and the candles on the tables are a nice touch."

"They are, but I figured you'd like the Christmas lights outside best of all." Aggie grinned as she spoke.

Since Aggie knew what happened on the porch a year-and-a-half ago, Doro rolled her eyes. "They look pretty." She cleared her throat. "I want to check the refreshment table before the big crowd gets here."

"I'll go with you," Aggie said, and the two friends left their beaus to mingle.

After a crowd gathered, Doro and Ev sat with Aggie and Wade at one of the tables ringing the dance floor. Mrs. Jones,

President Adams, and Floyd Quartine joined them. Casual conversation ensued until the music, again provided by students, began. Since a foxtrot was the first melody, Doro eagerly joined Ev, along with other couples. When that tune ended, another slow song followed, so they did not part until a man tapped Ev on the shoulder.

"Mind if I cut in?" Vance asked, a grin on his handsome face.

Since Ev looked like he minded, Doro hurried to reply. "Of course not." Ev's glare went from the other man to her. She squeezed his hand. "Why don't you ask Mrs. Jones to partner you? She and her husband used to cut quite a rug, so she'd enjoy it. You would, too."

A resigned sigh left him. "Sure thing."

For a moment, Doro watched Ev walk away. Everything in her demanded she call him back, but she couldn't. Dancing with others was a must and would be, even if she and Ev were engaged. One simply did not partner the same fellow for every song. Besides, this was an opportunity to chat with Vance. With real reluctance, she put one hand in Vance's and the other on his shoulder. When he would have pulled her closer, Doro resisted.

Vance winked at her. "Since you're not engaged, making Mallow jealous might do some good."

The suggestion that she needed to lure and snag Ev rankled. "No need for that."

"Judging from the expression on his face before he walked away, probably not."

With that, Vance swung Doro around the floor. She had to admit he was a fine dancer, as good as Ev, but she did not savor being in his arms. Only Ev evoked feelings of coming home.

Doro forced her mind off her sweetheart and back to the present. Perhaps she could learn something of value from Vance. At the very least, she ought to try. "I haven't seen your parents yet. They're coming tonight, aren't they? I hope the book being stolen hasn't upset your mother too much."

"She's been beside herself, but I assured her that it had to be a pledge prank. Both Father and I engaged in similar jokes when we were in college. It's not unusual, as we discussed earlier. I'm certain the hefty reward will move mountains, and I've let it be known to all the frat presidents that I'll serve as the go-between."

"Really? So, you'll get the book, return it to your parents, and take the money to the guilty party."

A chuckle rumbled out of him. "Guilty is a strong word. It was a prank."

Doro did not agree, but she followed his lead. "Although plenty of antics have occurred in the past, none has involved stealing something irreplaceable and invaluable."

"Which makes it quite a feat."

His reaction, especially considering his mother's distress, bothered Doro. "So, when do you expect the book to reappear?"

"To get the reward, it'll have to be returned by noon. I've let the fraternities know."

"The presidents all insist their pledges weren't involved."

Vance pulled back enough to look into Doro's face. "The copper told you that."

"Officer Mallow shared the information."

"I'm not surprised. In any case, why admit it when they might get in trouble with the college?"

"President Adams promised he wouldn't press charges, and your parents did the same." She made it a statement.

"I've heard you're an amateur sleuth, so I guess Mallow lets you in on his cases."

The amusement in his voice chafed. "I've worked on a few with him and Constable Lammers. Aggie has helped, too." Doro yearned to give chapter-and-verse of her sleuthing but resisted. "But how will the book get to you? Have you set a plan?"

"If I tell you, you'll tell Mallow," Vance replied. "Then, he and Lammers will set a trap."

"They're abiding by what President Adams wants. What your parents want. No charges will be filed." Ev and Wade might pursue answers without approval, but Doro did not reveal that. "I'm just curious."

His lips twitched. "I'll tell you this much. I expect to hear who has the book tonight. Then, I'll make arrangements to meet them. I'll keep it until the brunch, but let Adams and my folks know it's safe ahead of time."

The partial revelation gave Doro some information. "Was that what was discussed at your old fraternity house between practice and the game?"

All amusement left his expression. "I saw you trailing us. Not a clandestine move."

"I wasn't trying to be sneaky. I wanted to talk with Rud and Hank."

Several moments passed before he responded. "We wanted to see the old house and chat with the brothers. No ladies allowed. As far as the book, don't worry. I'm confident it'll turn up."

His neat sidestep gave Doro little choice but to comment on the last assertion. "As long as the book is back for the presentation, and it can be tucked into the library case afterward, I'm happy." But if the perpetrators were caught, she would be ecstatic. Doro considered pressing for more, but the song ended, and he grasped her elbow.

"Let's get you back to Mallow. He seems a serious sort, and I don't want to run afoul of the law."

Again, questions rose in Doro's mind. She would have voiced them if Ev had not crossed the floor to stand at her side. He took her.

"Let's get some refreshments," he said, his attention on her.

Vance released her free arm. "Thanks for the dance, Doro." He nodded at Ev. "Officer." Then, he strode away.

Doro spun to face Ev. "I wasn't finished talking to him."

A muscle jumped in Ev's jaw. "Sorry. I didn't realize the two of you were chatting so amiably."

She released a pent-up breath. "It wasn't necessarily amiable, but I got a little information."

Ev's dark lashes fluttered down. When he looked at her again, a flush rose in his cheeks. "Like I said already, I'm a jealous fool, so Wade isn't alone."

"There's no reason to be jealous," she assured him with a smile. When the music started again, Doro made a suggestion. "Let's dance or leave the floor. People are staring at us."

His nostrils flared with a sharp intake of breath. "Let's dance."

As she went into his arms, Doro felt the tension leave Ev. Peaking over his shoulder, she scanned the crowd. "No one is staring now."

"Good. There's been enough speculation about us among the men in Maple Hall. I don't need to fan the flames."

The comment caught her off-guard, and Doro leaned back to study his expression. "What do you mean?"

His color deepened. "Some professors can't believe we're a serious couple."

The explanation only increased her dismay. "They're gossiping about us?"

A rueful smile touched his lips. "Men engage in tittle-tattle."

"That's not a surprise, but it doesn't explain what you mean." Although Doro realized some people had gossiped about her relationship with Ev, especially after the Sweetheart Dance, most of the talk had been supportive. Townsfolk, who had known her all her life, were happy for Doro. The same was true for the other residents of Wheaton Hall. If male colleagues nattered about her and Ev, the talk had not gotten back to her. Only support had. Most speculation was in regard to the two of them getting engaged, but she did not want to say that. "Of course, people talked after we made it clear we were courting. That's generally regarded as a serious step."

"It is." As he spoke, his warm breath brushed her ear.

"I must be dense, but I don't understand what you mean by people not believing we're courting."

The hand at her waist tightened convulsively. "More than one male professor has asked me if I plan to get a degree."

Her head fell back as she stared at him. "What? Why would you do that?"

He took several deep breaths. "So, we'd be on a more equal footing."

Shock momentarily held her mute before realization hit hard. No wonder Ev had not talked about a betrothal. He feared he did not measure up. His comments about his lack of an advanced education troubled him. Doro intertwined their fingers. "You don't need a degree. If you want one, I'll be in your corner even though it'd mean we wouldn't have much time together. Two jobs and taking classes would keep you far too busy for stepping out. We don't do that as often as I'd like now." For long moments, Doro held her breath. Had she said the right things?

His expression remained stoic. "I wish I had more formal education, because I don't want to embarrass you."

Her jaw dropped. "Embarrass me. You make me proud. You're a fine man. A brave one, too. And smart. Not only that, you support me working. Many men wouldn't. Probably some of the ones who've given you a hard time are in that group." Doro knew a few male professors had stood against married women being employed at the college. Several lived in Maple Hall. How dare they insinuate Ev was not good enough for her? And clearly, that is what they had done.

Color again flared in his lean cheeks. "Yeah, that sounds about right."

Doro's heart clenched. "I've realized there's been gossip about Aggie and Wade—behind their backs and to his face, not hers. I should've known you're exposed to similar comments when it comes to schooling. Because it doesn't matter to me,

I haven't understood how it could bother you. It shouldn't, although that's probably easy for me to say."

"If I never earn a degree, we'll always have a gulf between us. You might not care now..." His voice ebbed away as the music ended. Ev released her and stepped back. "We can talk about this later. Right now, I'd like to know what Vance said that might help us find the book."

Although she wanted to pursue the topic of education, Doro agreed the case had to come first. "We can get refreshments and step outside," Doro suggested.

After they secured cups of punch, Doro and Ev moved to the large porch and found a bench in a secluded corner. "All right. What did he say?" Ev asked.

Disappointment stabbed Doro when Ev got down to business. So much for a romantic interlude before discussing progress. After summarizing her exchange with Vance, she paused. "What do you think?

He shrugged. "Hard to say for sure. He could be involved in the prank or just speculate, from experience, about who took it. After we split up at the ball field, I went back to Maple Hall and on to the office. I'm more and more inclined to believe a fraternity didn't initiate the theft, but one could be colluding with former members."

"I agree, and I also think Vance is involved. He's repeated his assertion that he was against offering a reward, but he's also mentioned it being a lure."

"And he, Ingram, and Devlin went to their old fraternity house."

"Exactly, but what about Lester? Can we clear him?" Doro hoped so.

"I stopped by his room after I got cleaned up. He's planning to come tonight, at least for a little while."

"Did he say how he got hurt?"

Ev nodded. "He helped one of the professors move a metal shelving unit. It had a raw edge that scraped him up and, when it started to tip, he grabbed for it and strained his wrist. Before you ask, I talked to the professor, and he confirmed the story. So, I agree with you that it's unlikely Jonson took the book."

Relief sang through Doro. "Good."

"I thought you'd be pleased, but Wade and I still want to find out who took it, even if we can't press charges."

Frustration echoed in his voice, and as Doro scanned Ev's face, she felt concern. Although he had shaved again and changed clothes, his weariness was obvious. "You're not planning to stay up and watch for a meeting between Vance and whoever has the book, are you? You barely got any rest last night."

"It's only this weekend. Things will be back to normal by Monday, and I'll catch up then."

"You'll be back to working two jobs and, with graduation coming soon, you will be busy."

His hand covered hers. "You'll be busy, too, and you got up early this morning to bring me coffee and sweets. You haven't rested since then, have you?"

"I had a chance to relax between leaving the ball game and getting ready for tonight. You've been on the go, and I worry about you."

"Thanks." He brushed a featherlight kiss to her temple before standing. "As far as what we're going to do, I'm not sure. There are plenty of places for young Smith to meet someone and keeping track of him, Ingram, and Devlin, not to mention the pledges, just in case they are responsible, is a tall order." He took a long breath. "We should get back inside. I'll tell Wade what Smith said, and we'll finagle some plan. No matter who took the manuscript, I want to catch them. Chances that the book will be sold have diminished, but we can't be sure. Besides, even if we don't lodge charges, I don't like not knowing who committed the act."

"As would I," Doro agreed. But Ev was right. Vance could meet the culprit in dozens of places, which hampered solving the case.

⁕

The next few hours passed quickly. Doro danced with Ev several more times, but she also stepped on the floor with a number of other fellows—colleagues, former classmates, and retired professors. She always kept track of Ev, who only danced with older ladies—much to Doro's pleasure. At the same time, she watched Rud, Vance, and the Devlins. All of them appeared to enjoy the evening. Vance asked her to dance again, and Rud followed suit. Both Lester and Hank kept their distance, which made Doro uneasy. Why would they stay away from her? Guilty consciences? Lester had a good excuse, but he could have stolen the book and also, hurt himself helping the professor.

Since she and Rud partnered for the jitterbug, she had little chance to quiz him. The same was true for her second dance with Vance. Doro noticed Aggie joined Rud for the Lindy Hop. Not much chance of conversation between them, either.

Shortly before midnight, people began to leave. Rud Ingram was among the first, but he stopped at the refreshment table to chat with Bonnie Adler. Seeing the pair together jogged Doro's memory, and she watched them closely. When Aggie took a seat next to her, Doro glanced at her friend. "Bonnie and Rud are talking."

"Interesting," Aggie murmured.

Doro had no time to reply because Stuart Adler strode up to the pair. Even from a distance, his anger was palpable. As he pulled his daughter back, the baker faced Rud. While the men's voices were loud, their words were not distinct.

"Let's calm them down," Aggie said before starting across the floor.

Doro followed but, by the time the friends reached the two men, Ev and Wade had stepped in.

"Stu, step back," Wade said.

"You too, Ingram. There's no need to make a scene," Ev added.

Although Adler did as Wade suggested, Rud moved away from the lawmen. "I didn't do anything. The old man came in and started making ugly accusations. Typical."

Anger flashed in the older man's gaze. "Leave my girl alone."

"She isn't a girl," Rud shot back. "She's a woman, so she doesn't have to listen to you."

"She'll do as I say while she's under my roof," Adler said.

"Pa, please," Bonnie murmured. "You're creating a scene."

A stricken expression blanketed the baker's face. "This man stole your brother's car from us, and you're being nice to him. I'd like to know why."

"Stu, why don't you and Bonnie discuss that later," Wade suggested before turning toward Rud. "As for you, why don't you leave?"

For a moment, Rud looked like he would object. Then, he turned back to Bonnie and winked. "I'll be seeing you."

Bonnie offered a tremulous grin. "You will."

As soon as Rud was out of earshot, Aggie addressed the younger woman. "Why don't you and your dad leave? You were planning to get the trays and such tomorrow anyhow."

"You're right. He's probably tired, so we should go. I'll come over after church." Bonnie's voice was a trembling whisper. She hurried away.

Adler looked from Wade to Ev. "Sorry. She had a crush on him years ago, and I guess even knowing he stole her brother's car hasn't put a damper on it."

"Like Doro said, you have to be tired after getting up early to bake. Go on home, Stu," Wade said.

Adler nodded before slowly tracing his daughter's steps.

He was barely out of sight when the band struck up another tune, and the remaining guests turned back to the floor. Although Doro would have enjoyed a last dance with Ev, she gave up the idea. "I wonder about Bonnie and Rud. He visited the bakery often when he was a student, but she was too young for him. Fifteen when he was twenty-one."

"He probably flirted and maybe got free baked goods. That would be like him," Aggie said.

"That and their exchange just now puts a new light on what Bonnie told you this morning," Ev observed.

"I agree," Doro said. "I knew she lived in Toledo, mostly with Inez. Now, I wonder if she saw Rud there."

"I do, too," Aggie put in.

Ev ran a hand over his face. "She heard voices in the middle of the night but couldn't—or wouldn't—identify them. What if she's part of the collusion?"

"It's possible." Doro shared what Vance had revealed during their dance.

A hollow sigh escaped Ev. "He knows more than he's admitting."

Wade frowned. "Yep, he sure does."

"Maybe going over some details would lead us to possible meeting places," Doro suggested. "One may already be set."

"If you two can leave, let's talk outside," Wade said to the young women.

After the two girlfriends agreed about not staying later, the entire group left the building. They walked twenty feet to where two benches faced each other and sat down.

When Doro leaned back, Ev laid his arm behind her shoulders. His warmth reached out to envelope her, and she relaxed against him. Peace filled her despite the questions rattling through her mind. "We talked about collusion, and I think it's more likely than ever after what we've learned."

"I agree, but how many people are complicit?" Ev asked.

"That's the question of the hour," Wade put in. "Doro talked to young Smith and Ingram tonight, and Aggie talked with Ingram, too. I tried to strike up a conversation with Devlin, but he had little to say."

"He danced only with his wife all night, which is unusual," Aggie said.

"It is," Doro agreed.

A harrumph left Wade. "I understand because I didn't want to dance with anyone except Aggie." He slid an arm around her waist, and she laid her head on his shoulder.

"Same here," Ev put in.

Doro shifted so she could see his face. "You wanted to dance with Aggie all night?"

Laughter left Ev. "You know I only want to dance with you."

"Good," she murmured before forcing herself back to the topic at hand. "We already talked about Rud, Hank, and Vance working together—maybe with their old fraternity. What if they promised the brothers a cut of the reward for snatching the book? Some clues point to the possibility." Doro reviewed sighting the trio with others as they headed to their old fraternity house.

Wade stretched his legs out. "If they split the reward with the house, everyone comes out ahead. At least that would be their perspective."

"It would, I'm sure," Ev muttered. "Who cares that all of us have been running around trying to solve the crime?"

"That sums it up," Wade agreed.

"Only if I'm right," Doro said. "We can't be sure I am."

"But your idea makes sense," Aggie said.

Ev's fingers played with the ends of Doro's sleek bob. "With young Smith as the go-between, anything is possible."

"True, but Adams will want to know which fraternity took it, if Vance puts the blame there. Whether or not he penalizes them is an open query. On top of that, Hank or Rud could've stolen the book, and then all agreed to tag pledges." Doro pointed out. "Or does that seem far-fetched?"

"It seems brilliant and possible," Aggie said. "Then, Vance, Hank, and Rud could split the reward and get a whole lot more. But what about Bonnie? Do you think she's somehow involved?"

"Hard to say," Doro responded. "What do you guys think?"

"Any of those groupings are possible, including Bonnie knowing what happened, which I think is more likely than her participating in the robbery," Ev said.

"I'd go along with that," Wade put in. "We're down to three primary suspects—Ingram, Devlin, and Smith. Devlin may not be involved although him talking with Ingram at the ball field leads to his likely participation. As for Bonnie, I'd say she may know what happened after the fact. And the pledges are in the mix."

Ev stopped twirling Doro's hair and sat up straighter. "Young Smith is staying at the President's house, so watching it is our best bet as far as catching the culprit."

"He said the deadline to return it is noon, but they won't meet in broad daylight," Doro said. The others agreed.

"So, Wade and I need to stake out Adams' home overnight," Ev put in.

"We do," the constable concurred.

"When you see the book being passed, what will you do?" Aggie asked. "President Adams didn't want charges pressed, and neither do the Smiths."

"Maybe they suspect their son's involvement," Ev said.

The assertion hung in the air for a long moment before Doro responded. "I wouldn't be surprised. Nor would it be strange if a fraternity gets the blame, which they'd probably take as credit, and a share of the money."

"Several possibilities remain on the table," Aggie said. "At least we're pretty sure the book will be returned."

As she listened, Doro considered what would happen after the book was safely back. "What about repercussions? Breaking into College Hall, smashing the showcase, and stealing the manuscript are all crimes. Can you charge anyone for damages?" In the light of a nearby street lamp, Doro noted the varying expressions. The lawmen looked tense while Aggie seemed anxious. "Maybe, like with the lost exam, holding to the letter of the law isn't as important as solving the problem."

Ev and Wade turned to one another. For long moments, neither spoke. Aggie eventually broke the silence. "You two will always do what's best. Doro and I know that."

Wade took her hand and lifted it to his lips. "What's best and what's right aren't necessarily the same. I can see that now."

When Ev remained silent, Doro laid her palm on his shoulder. "What do you think?" Even though, as head constable, Wade would make the final decision on whether or not to close the case, Ev deserved his say.

He caught her hand and brought it to his lips. "The three things you mentioned are all crimes."

"So, you plan to dig into how it happened in order to charge Rud and Vance and maybe Hank, despite the Smiths and President Adam's preference?" Doro said. "Possibly Bonnie or fraternity pledges, too. Or even Lester if he's involved? No one promised to ignore the damage to the showcase, did they?"

Ev's gaze went around the group before again resting on Doro. "No, but the Smiths will likely pay for it to be fixed, and whoever is guilty will eventually face justice in some way or another. I don't have to be the one to mete it out."

Doro lightly brushed his smooth cheek before letting her hand drop to her side. "I know that's hard for you."

"I can be a little too regimented," Ev admitted, "and your take on this case has made me understand why your father and President Adams didn't have Lester and his sister charged for breaking, entering, and stealing. The end result, getting the test back and Aggie keeping her scholarship, were most important."

"I'm glad you think so," Doro said.

"It's not easy for us lawmen to go along with no charges, but I'm with Ev on this. If a fraternity is involved, President Adams will handle them. As for the others who may be involved, if they're fingered, they might not do something similar again," Wade said.

"Agreed," Ev said.

Doro glanced from one lawman to the other. "You'll let the guilty party feel uneasy going forward."

"Yep," Ev agreed. "Scrutiny can keep people from causing more trouble."

A chuckle left Aggie. "It often works with students."

Wade looked at his watch before standing up. "I want to walk Aggie home and change my clothes before we stake out Adams' house. What time do you want to meet there, Ev?"

Before he could speak, Doro inserted a comment. "Vance promised to go back to the house with his parents, so he'll have to sneak out after everyone is asleep."

"How do you know that?" Ev inquired.

"He mentioned it when we were dancing the second time." Doro shared what he had told her. "His mother was afraid he and some friends might drive into the city. Vance chuckled over it because she actually mentioned how things don't get going at speakeasies until after midnight, especially on the weekend."

A chuckle left Aggie. "How would she know?"

"Vance lives at home off-and-on," Doro said. "I suppose she watches his activities."

"Evidently." Aggie stood up and put her hand in the crook of Wade's arm. "That will give our fellows a little breathing room."

"How about us meeting at the office around one-thirty? It's after midnight now, and they aren't apt to settle down for at least a half-hour, maybe longer," Wade asked Ev. "Young Smith will likely not go to his meeting until the middle of the night."

"Or even close to dawn from what he said," Doro put in.

"Let's still meet at one-thirty," Ev said. "We don't want to miss him taking off."

After saying their farewells, Aggie and Wade headed toward Wheaton Hall. When they were out of earshot, Doro sighed. "This is really pleasant, but you might be able to grab some sleep if you walk me home now."

"I'd rather sit here with my arm around you, but Tee needs to get out. She's back at my place, since Wade's kids are going to his sister's house after church tomorrow. We could get her and take a walk."

"That sounds lovely, as long as I can change my shoes."

"We'll get our dog," Ev said. "I'll change mine, and we'll go to your place for you to change."

"Perfect," Doro said.

Doro and Ev turned toward the men's faculty residence hall. Her spirit felt lighter than it had for days. Fresh delight filled her when Ev and Tee joined her in the front hall. The little dog danced merrily as Doro petted her head.

"She's happy to see you," Ev remarked as they headed outside.

"I always miss her when we're apart."

Ev took her hand. "I feel the same when I don't see you."

The warmth of his palm sent shivers through her. "Summer vacation is coming, and we'll both have free time." As she spoke, Doro thought they'd be together even more if they married. Did Ev think about that? His reply referred to marriage, but not theirs.

"I might be taking on the constable's job, at least temporarily. Wade and Aggie haven't set a date, but they may soon. I told him I'd step in while they're away."

"Aggie hasn't mentioned a summer wedding."

"Wade hasn't, either. I just let him know I'm more available then, and Aggie has time off school. It's up to them when they tie the knot. I'm just saying, if they do it soon, I'll be busy."

His words confused her, so Doro moved the conversation to a more benign topic. "It's a beautiful night. Why don't we walk through the park after I change?"

"Sure. Tee would like that."

At their first stop, Maple Hall, Ev put on walking shoes and scooped up Tee. When they reached Wheaton Hall, Doro rushed upstairs and donned more casual footwear and a less fancy outfit. Within minutes, she rejoined Ev and Tee, and the group went back out into the night.

Chapter Ten

The park, which sat at the south side of town not far from the campus, had well-lit paths, while benches sat at various positions throughout. Towering oaks, maples, elms, and black walnuts were scattered in clumps, and small shrubs lined many of the walkways. "The park is pretty, even at night. I'm glad the council decided to install electric lampposts a few years back."

"They put in more, now that the pool is almost finished," Ev observed.

"I can't wait to see it," Doro said. "All the children in Michaw are excited. A few went to Sylvania to swim in their pool, but most made do wading in the creek."

"It's a great addition to the town," Ev agreed. "I never learned how to swim myself. What about you?"

"I learned in Colorado when my dad and I first visited my mom out there. Since then, I've been to the pool in Sylvania, which was built a couple years ago. It'll be lovely to have one here. I'm sure you'll learn quickly."

"If I have time," he murmured.

As they continued on, she gestured to look at the memorial plaque that had been dedicated two years earlier. "I'm glad they included everyone who has served, not just those who died in wars."

"I'm glad, too. Plenty of men came home injured beyond measure, sometimes with wounds we don't see."

"They do," Doro said, as she thought about Sam Adler. Would his parents ever get their money back? Or was Stu Adler confused? Again, she wondered about Rud, his debts, and the missing book.

"Let's head over to where the pool is going in. It's supposed to open on Memorial Day, so progress should be noticeable."

"I'd like to see it."

The pair, along with Tee who led the way, continued to the far end of the park. Doro relished the feel of her soft hand in Ev's callused one. She contemplated resurrecting their discussion of the male professors who had been snide to him. Figuring out how to approach the topic was a conundrum, so she walked silently beside him.

When they reached a place where post lights had been erected, but were not all on, he spoke. "We need to watch where we're going, since it's dimmer over this way. With the construction, there could be ruts. It's good you changed your shoes, but you could still turn your ankle."

Doro chuckled. Her low-heeled, lace-up Oxfords were serviceable, but she clasped his hand tighter. "I'll lean on you."

"Good." The single word echoed with emotion, but he said nothing more.

The lamps near the pool area provided enough illumination to see concrete had been poured as decking, and about a foot of water filled the deepest part. The shallow end, which was closest to her, was not visible from her vantage point although the cement surround indicated where it stopped. "It's a nice size."

"It is," Ev agreed.

Before he could say more, Tee yanked hard on the lead. Doro tried to hold her back, but the little dog darted toward the pool. "Oh, no. She's so curious. What if she falls in and hits the concrete bottom?" The little dog could be seriously injured, or worse. The idea made Doro sick at heart.

Ev whistled, but Tee kept running. Both of them called out with the same response from the dog. "I'll get her." With that, he dashed off.

Doro followed suit, but she lagged behind Ev and Tee. By the time she reached the pool edge, the little dog was barking wildly and lunging toward something laying on the pool's downslope from the shallow to the deep end. "What's wrong with her?"

"I don't know. She's intent on whatever is near the shallow end. I can't see exactly what it is. Maybe some trash. Or an animal. I hope it isn't an injured raccoon, because Tee would come out on the bad end of any battle with one. I'll have to get closer and climb down. Otherwise, I won't be able to grab her leash."

While Ev shed his shoes and rolled up his pant legs, he kept talking to the little dog, who continued to yip and jump around.

Although Tee was always energetic, her behavior was unusual. Why was she so agitated? Doro watched Ev and Tee. She saw him move into the pool and bend down. The dog disappeared, only to resurface dragging a man's shoe along. A very distinctive shoe. A brown spectator wing-tip. One hand flew to her mouth as a gasp escaped her. Over the last few days, Doro had seen two people with that type of footwear: Rud and Hank. Her heart raced and her breathing grew rapid. "Who is it?" A seemingly endless void preceded his reply.

Ev bowed his head. "Ingram."

Doro's pulse pounded. "Is he all right?"

After turning to look over his shoulder at Doro, Ev shook his head. "No. He's dead."

Shivers rippled through Doro, and she wrapped her arms around her waist to quell them. Forming words proved impossible, so she stood staring into the pool where Rud laid at an awkward angle. His head was toward the deep end, while his torso was on the downslope. As Doro gained control, she struggled to study the body with dispassion. Both feet were well above his head, and one still had a shoe on.

Ev's voice intruded on her musings. "Will you find Wade and tell him what happened? He and Aggie may still be in the reception room at Wheaton Hall. He'll want to contact Doc Silven, I'm sure. I'll stay here to make sure the scene isn't disturbed."

"Of course," Doro murmured. Shock slowed her thought process. "Do you want me to take Tee?" The dog had dropped the shoe at Doro's feet but raced back to Ev.

"I doubt if she'll leave, so go ahead. We'll be waiting."

"I'll hurry." Doro darted out of the park. Some homes were dark, but a few had lights on. The darkness did not bother her, but knowing Rud laid dead in the park did. She hurried on and encountered Wade walking away from the women's faculty residence. Evidently, he and Aggie had lingered, just as Ev thought, and who could blame them. They were deeply in love and every moment together was precious.

"Where is Ev?" Concern roughened his voice. "What's wrong? You two didn't see young Smith out-and-about already, did you?"

After explaining what happened, Doro finished with, "We could call Doc from inside." She gestured toward the women's faculty residence.

"Good idea, and I'll contact President Adams. He should know, since Ingram is a college visitor. You'll have to unlock the door for me."

Doro hurriedly did so, and the pair stepped inside. Aggie, only partway up the staircase, turned to look at them, surprise etched on her face. "What happened? Is Ev okay? What about little Tee? Where are they?"

While Doro explained, her friend descended the steps. "That's awful. What happened to Rud that he ended up in the pool?"

"I'm not sure. Maybe he fell in while taking a walk," Doro replied.

As soon as Wade finished his calls, he turned to the women. "I'm heading over there. I'll see you two later."

"I'm going back," Doro insisted.

Wade shook his head. "You can stay here with Aggie."

"No. At the very least, I need to get Tee," Doro replied. When Wade hesitated, she rushed on. "Aggie and I won't get in the way."

He chuckled. "Now, both of you are coming?"

"Of course," Aggie said with a smile. "I'm changing first."

"I'll wait here for you," Doro put in.

"I'm going now," Wade said. "The two of you should be safe together, but be careful on your way back to the park."

The two friends agreed they would be cautious before Aggie dashed upstairs. Within minutes, she was back and they headed out.

"Rud left a little early," Aggie said. "Maybe he met someone in the park, but who?"

"That's a good question because, if he went there to see someone else, it could've involved the manuscript. Earlier, it sounded like he planned to see Bonnie again, although maybe not tonight. As for Vance, Rud wouldn't have met him so early."

"My thoughts, too. But it could also be that Rud took a walk. When we danced, I noticed alcohol on his breath. I didn't mention it to Wade since he wasn't happy about me dancing with Rud. It was the Lindy Hop, so I wasn't close to him. But the smell of booze was potent."

"I also danced with him, but I didn't notice his breath."

"You two were on the floor more than an hour before he and I were."

"A good point. If he was drinking, he could've mis-stepped and fallen into the pool." She had already considered the possibility.

"Let's hope that's what happened."

"It would be better than some alternatives," Doro agreed.

After a short walk, the two friends were at the pool where they found their beaus in deep discussion. Tee, who was sitting at Ev's feet, ran to greet the young women. Doro bent to pet the little dog's sleek head. "You need your paws washed, girl."

"And a treat," Aggie said as she scratched Tee's chin. "Finding a body was good work."

Her friend's comments and Tee's delight at the attention made Doro smile, despite the circumstances. "It was wonderful work, because Ev and I might not have noticed the body without Tee racing over here. You're a doggie detective."

The men joined the women in time to hear the last remarks. "She is," Ev agreed. "You're right, Doro. We probably would've passed by and missed the body without Tee alerting us."

Doro studied Ev and Wade. Their feet were bare, and their pant legs were wet above the rolls at their ankles. "You got a bit damp."

"We did because there's a couple inches of water," Ev replied.

"Can you tell how Rud died?" Doro asked.

The men exchanged a long look before Wade answered. "Doc Silven is on his way. He can make a determination, although probably only after he does a thorough examination. That'll be in his office."

Doro focused on Ev. "You had time to study the body. Don't you have a gut feeling?"

The words were barely out of her mouth when two figures emerged from the darkness. One was President Adams and the other was Doc Silven. The former had not changed out of his party togs, but the physician looked like he had emerged from bed. Although clad in a shirt, jacket, pants, and boots, his hair was standing on end.

After an exchange of greetings, Silven looked from Doro to Ev. "You two found the body?"

They explained about Tee leading them to it, and Ev offered details. "Wade and I looked more closely. Ingram is where the shallow end goes into the deep part. Ingram's head is toward the bottom, but not in the water, which isn't deep."

"Probably from the heavy rain mid-week," Silven suggested.

"I'd say so, Doc," Wade agreed.

The conversation disturbed Doro. "Plenty of our visitors expressed an interest in the new pool, so Rud might've taken a detour after leaving the dance. Maybe he tripped and fell forward a ways." She did not add a few drinks could have led to that possibility.

Aggie nodded. "Is that possible?"

"It is, but we can't say for sure," Wade replied. "Both Ev and I were in the pool and looked closely although we didn't touch the body." He turned to the physician. "We wanted you to see him first."

"Thanks. It may help determine what happened." Doc glanced at Ev. "You had time to study the situation. Anything stand out?"

"It looks like Ingram hit his head, since there's a big contusion," Ev replied.

"So, it wasn't murder," President Adams observed. He looked around the group. "I'm only wondering because we've had more than one in the area, as you all know."

Had Rud fallen into the pool or had he been pushed? If the latter was true, who was the culprit and was the death linked to the stolen book? Doro waited to hear what else Ev had to say.

"It isn't clear." Ev glanced at Doro before continuing. "Doc's expertise will help make a determination."

"I understand," the college president said. "It's just that I've heard Dr. Ingram argued with other alumni and a shop-keeper." His gaze went to Wade.

"And with me," the constable said in his usual amiable tone. "But I can account for my whereabouts all evening, and I have witnesses."

Adams put both hands up. "I wasn't making an allegation, Wade. Not at all, but Dr. Ingram has been a problem during his visit. I haven't told anyone else, but Hank Devlin and his wife accused Rudyard of stealing the book."

"When was that?" Doro asked in surprise.

"They took me off to one side before leaving the dance," Adams replied, "so, I haven't had a chance to tell anyone. I was tied up with the Smiths when all of you left, or I would've mentioned it then. I've been with them ever since. When Wade called, we were still talking over what to do if the book doesn't show up by the time brunch begins." He looked at the constable. "I planned to call you as soon as they went to bed."

Wade nodded. "The Devlins left a little early, didn't they?"

"She had a headache," Adams said, "so, they took off right after Rudyard did. Vance Smith left and came back because he wanted to speak with Dr. Ingram outside, or so he said. They were friends in college and evidently, stayed in touch."

Anxiety prickled along Doro's spine as she thought back to the dance attendees. She did not want to blurt out accusations, so she resolved to later ask Ev, Aggie, and Wade what they had noticed. "Is Vance at your house?"

"He's the one who answered the telephone," the administrator replied. "He was icoming downstairs when it rang."

That struck Doro as odd, so she made another query. "Still dressed?"

"Yes, he was, but he'd taken time to change," Adams said. "Vance wanted to come along, but I asked him to stay at the house."

"Thanks," Wade put in. "Did you tell him what happened?"

With one hand, Adams brushed an errant lock of hair from his face. "I simply said there was an issue concerning the college."

"Good," Ev murmured. "We don't want gossip spreading or anyone else coming here." When a shiver rippled through Ev, he wrapped his arms around his lean waist.

Doc Silven stepped closer to the pool. "I'd like to take a look before we move him. I'll need help to do that. I put on old clothes and brought boots."

"I'm already wet, so I can assist you," Ev said.

"I'll lend a hand, if needed," Adams added.

Doro also volunteered. "I can join in."

Ev shot her a dubious glance. "That won't be necessary."

"Aggie and I aren't in our party clothes," Doro pointed out.

"I see, but we don't want to disturb the scene," Ev replied. "Although Wade and I looked, Doc might be able to tell us more. Besides, that water is cold, and we have to stand in it to see the body. There's no sense in extra people getting chilled and wet."

Doro noted that he did not mention ladies, in particular, so she agreed. "All right."

Over the next ten minutes, Doc Silven studied the situation up close and talked to Ev and Wade, but their voices didn't carry. During that time, President Adams stood with Doro and Aggie. "Doc was smart to bring a flashlight, so he could get a better look," he said. "I didn't think of it."

"Neither did we," Doro admitted. Her primary interest had been getting back to Ev. So much for always sleuthing. His well-being took precedence over everything else.

Doc Silven climbed out of the pool. "I think Ev is right about Dr. Ingram striking his head, probably as he fell into the pool. Whether or not his tumble was accidental from a fall or intentional from being struck, I can't say. Even after a thorough examination in my office, I won't know how he landed in the pool."

"Will you do a blood alcohol test?" Doro asked. "We have some indication he'd been drinking." She did not name Aggie as the witness.

"Sure, I can do that," Doc agreed. "I did many as an intern in the city, and I have the equipment."

"That'd help," Ev observed. "I tried to get fingerprints from the lavatory window and the showcase, but the thief must've worn gloves."

The comment made Doro realize she had not asked about him taking prints. So much else had happened.

"Let's get him out, so you can at least study the body," Wade said.

"I brought a stretcher, so I'll get it," Silven said.

"I'll help you," President Adams put in. With that, he followed the physician.

When the pair returned, Ev and Doc clambered back into the pool with the stretcher. A few minutes passed before they climbed up to where Wade and President Adams could assist. At the sight of Rud's body, Doro reached out for Aggie's hand. Her friend clung to it like it was a lifeline. Although Aggie had cut ties with Rud long ago, seeing his dead body had to affect her. It affected Doro, who swallowed hard against the rising tide of sadness.

Ev turned to the physician. "I didn't want to search his pockets before you got here, but I'd like to do it now."

"Good idea," Silven replied.

While Ev search Rud's jacket and pants, Doro averted her gaze. When Wade spoke, she looked back.

"What's that?" the constable asked.

Ev unfolded a piece of paper that he had pulled from a coat pocket. "A note. The writing is slightly blurred, but it looks like someone is planning to meet Ingram later today."

"What does it say?" Doro inquired as she stepped forward.

"*Meet me by the war memorial at four o'clock this morning and bring the book. If you don't show up, I'll go to the cops about your nefarious activities over the last couple of years. Come alone and don't tell anyone.*" Ev handed the note to Wade. "What do you think?"

"Someone will be in the park expecting to see Ingram, and that person is ready to blackmail him for something, which is impossible now."

President Adams studied the man on the ground. "Rudyard was a good student, and I'm sorry this happened. So sorry." He looked around the group. "Now, I wonder if another of our graduates planned to get the stolen book from him to reap the reward."

"It seems that way," Doc observed. "I'll leave figuring that out to our lawmen. Now, I want to get the body to my house and begin a thorough examination."

"I'll go along and help carry the stretcher," Adams said.

"Thank you," Silven replied.

Before leaving, Doc assured the two lawmen that he would telephone as soon as the cause of death was determined. "I can finish tonight and not miss my office hours in the morning, so expect a call in a few hours, maybe less. Someone will be in the constable's office by then, right?"

"Either Ev or I will be there until close to four," Wade assured him.

The comment put Doro on edge. Of course, the lawmen would want to catch the blackmailer, but how? After Silven and Adams departed, she glanced at Ev. "You didn't find a flask?"

Ev shook his head. "None was on him, but what makes you think he was drinking?"

After a quick glance at her friend, Doro shrugged. "Alcohol was on his breath during the dance."

"If he had a flask, he could've left it somewhere or gotten booze from another person," Wade observed. "Doc should have some information for us after blood work."

"Let's go to your office and wait," Ev suggested. "We can talk more there."

Chapter Eleven

After arriving at the office, Wade and Aggie made coffee. Within minutes, the group was settled with cups of the fragrant brew. Doro and Aggie took chairs across from Wade while Ev pulled another one up. Tee curled at his feet and went to sleep.

A chuckle escaped Ev. "We've worn her out. Finding a body and retrieving a shoe almost her size was hard work."

"She's small but mighty. Now, she's entitled to rest." All of them could use sleep, but Doro bit back the idea. Work remained. A lot of work.

Wade put a notepad and pencil on his desk. "We need to think about the note and who wrote it. Since it references the book, I'd like to discuss the culprit or culprits before moving on."

"Good idea," Ev agreed.

"I still think Doro's idea on Ingram and his buddy Smith, and maybe Devlin, going for the reward is a good one," Wade said. "But we know Smith wasn't in the park tonight."

"Which may point to Rud meeting someone else," Doro said. "Bonnie Adler, for example. Remember how he said he'd see her."

Ev's forehead furrowed. "People say that often."

"I was watching her when he did," Doro clarified, "and she looked happy, even excited."

Aggie nodded. "I noticed that, too, and Rud winked like they were sharing a secret."

Wade ran his fingers through his hair. "The girl is smitten. Even us old guys could see that, but would she leave his body? Wouldn't she want to get help?"

"I'm not sure about that," Doro said. "Maybe Rud was alone and fell into the pool due to being intoxicated."

"We shouldn't assume anything. Doc will check his blood alcohol level. Those tests are fairly accurate, especially if Ingram consumed a lot of liquor," Ev observed. "Right now, we should focus on the note writer. It's unlikely that person followed Ingram, and less likely he came so early."

Wade took another sip of coffee. "The note writer is also a blackmailer, who must've passed a note because he didn't have a chance to talk with Rud in private. Or maybe he had someone else pass the note. If another person passed it, he or she could've read it and followed Rud from the dance."

"That makes sense," Aggie said. "But getting back to Bonnie, remember Micah mentioned a man and a woman, or a boy, out last night. Since it could've been Rud and Bonnie, they might've made plans to meet again tonight, especially in light of their last words at the dessert table."

Doro nodded. "I agree."

"I still wonder about her not going for help if she saw him fall into the pool," Wade observed.

"You'd think so, but maybe not, especially if she knew he was dead. After all, meeting him alone would upset her father and ruin her reputation," Doro said.

"You're right on both counts," Aggie added. "But she wouldn't have hurt Rud. Not if she's had a crush for all these years."

For a moment, Doro mulled over her friend's assessment. "She could've gotten angry if he put her off. Bonnie wants to go back to the city. What if Rud mentioned marriage?"

"Which is possible," Aggie said. "Or he hinted at it and didn't follow-through. That'd be upsetting."

Ev drummed his fingers on the chair arms. "You two are suggesting the girl might've pushed him and, after he fell into the pool, took off."

After shifting toward him, Doro studied his expression. While she was not sure about the theory, she wondered about his opinion. "Do you think it's impossible?"

"Not at all. It is a valid consideration," Ev said. "People often act out when they're hurt or angry."

Wade rolled the pencil between his broad palms. "Since Bonnie seemed smitten with Ingram, it's possible. She and Stu left early, so there was time between them leaving and when you found the body."

"Because I went to my place and changed," Doro said. "Mr. Adler rose early, like he does every Monday through Saturday, to bake, he might've gone straight to bed as soon as they got home. Then, Bonnie could've left to meet Rud."

"Important details, but others might've followed Rud. That could've been Devlin or even Jonson," Wade said.

"None of which helps us pinpoint the note writer." Frustration underscored Ev's words. "We need to set a plan to do that."

The telephone ringing interrupted the conversation. "That's gotta be Doc," Wade said as he moved to the counter and answered.

Hearing one side of the conversation didn't help much, but Doro still listened intently. On either side of her, Ev and Aggie did the same. When Wade returned to his desk, he released a long sigh.

"First, Doc thinks Rud Ingram hit the side of his head when he fell, just as we suspected at the scene. That being said, it could've been accidental. Doc reiterated not being sure. He's working on the blood alcohol test next."

Doro slumped back in her chair. "Then, it's fifty-fifty that it's accidental or intentional."

"Exactly right," Aggie said, "so, we still have questions."

Doro perched on the edge of her chair. "When did someone give him the note? I keep wondering."

Several seconds of silence passed before Ev responded. "The note was probably passed at the dance. As far as who gave it to him, that could've been any of a few people. Again, I think we need to move forward and set a plan to trap the note writer. That's the only way to find out for sure who it is."

"You're right," Wade agreed. "We can catch him and find out about the blackmail and what he knows about the book theft. After Doc gives us the final report, we'll know more about what caused Ingram to fall into the pool. As for the book, young

Smith will get it. Unfortunately, with these other developments, we can't watch Adams' house until after four o'clock."

"I hate for you to disturb the President again, but he might be amenable to sitting up and watching to see if Vance goes out," Doro said. "He may still be awake, so I could call."

"Probably wise," Ev concurred.

"It is," Wade added.

After telephoning the President, Doro returned to the group. "He says he wouldn't sleep much anyhow, so he'll station himself in the front parlor where he can see the staircase and the door."

"That'll help," Ev said. "Now, about setting a trap."

While she could not disagree with the idea, Doro felt a surge of alarm. Trapping a blackmailer could be dangerous. "Can I see the paper?" The query was mainly a stalling technique.

Ev pulled it out of his pocket and handed it to her. "What do you think?"

"It's print, not longhand," Doro murmured.

"And that's notable because..." Ev's voice trailed off.

"Thinking about the target of your trap might be useful. Some people are less likely to fight back than others," Doro observed. For several moments, Ev's gaze met hers. Doro thought he might object, but he finally nodded.

"So, what about the writing?" he asked.

"When I spoke with Bonnie, she was writing a note for the neighbor. I complimented her handwriting, and she beamed. Then, she went on to say how she'd won penmanship awards every year in school. She also said her dad prints, almost illegibly," Doro replied.

"If she's the note writer, and I'm not sure about that, she wouldn't have tried to disguise her writing?" Ev asked.

"It's not easy, especially for someone who writes beautifully like Bonnie does. Besides, I doubt if Rud has seen her handwriting enough to recognize it," Doro said.

"An astute observation," Ev told her with a grin.

"It is," Wade agreed. "Do we know of anyone who prints?"

Aggie's brow wrinkled as if she was in deep concentration. "Lester's right wrist was taped due to that injury, so that might affect his writing. I know he isn't a top suspect, but we talked about him earlier."

"We did, and I agree he could've written the note," Doro said.

"Pain would affect his penmanship," Ev commented.

"So, Lester could be the blackmailer," Aggie suggested. After the group agreed, she moved on. "We haven't seen Hank's writing."

Doro shifted restlessly in her chair. "Hank was out last night so he may have seen the thief, evidently Rud, leaving College Hall."

After jotting more notes, Aggie tapped her pencil against the paper pad. "He and Cereta also know a little about what Rud's been doing for the past couple of years."

"They do, and Vance must, too," Doro put in. "As far as his penmanship, I know nothing."

"But we can't rule him out," Ev stated, "even though I see him more of a conspirator than a blackmailer."

Following a scan of her notes, Aggie agreed. "I've got Vance and Hank at the top of my list. It could be Lester, though, or even Mr. Adler. How do we figure out which one plans to meet Rud?"

"By setting and springing a trap, like I suggested," Ev replied.

When Aggie looked as dubious as Doro felt, she offered a suggestion. "We could create a dummy to sit on the bench at the memorial and put a coat on it. Otherwise, the note writer might expect to see the book laying out."

"The coat is a good idea, and it's cool enough now for a light one," Wade said.

Ev sat straight up. "I agree on a coat, but not the dummy. There are two post lamps on either side of the panel. The note writer would see it wasn't a real person too soon."

"That's a definite problem," Wade said. "There are several massive silver maples around the memorial, along with a stand of birches. Whoever's coming will likely conceal himself as long as possible."

"My thought, too," Ev said. "Since I'm about the same height and build as Ingram, I can be the decoy. A coat will conceal any small differences in our weights, and eye color wouldn't be discernable at night."

Anxiety whirled through Doro. This was exactly what she wanted to avoid—Ev putting himself in harm's way. Again. "If the person plans to hide between trees, which seems probable, he may also plan to attack Rud. But now, not Rud. You." Ev reached for her hand, but she snatched it back. "Besides, your hair is much darker."

"I'll wear a hat," Ev said.

Doro did not relent. "You were shot in August, poisoned last May, and shot a year-and-a-half ago right before you came here. Surely, you don't plan to be a sitting duck now."

With two fingers, he massaged his temple. "Should I mention you and Aggie were held in a cellar at Christmas about sixteen months ago? Or about you being kidnapped from a train last summer?"

A tense silence permeated the room while Doro stared back at him. "It's not the same. You're deliberately putting yourself in danger." She turned to Wade. "Don't you agree with me?"

Before the constable could reply, Ev did. "Wade and I will be armed. He'll be there watching. Besides, we're lawmen. We have experience in these matters, and we'll proceed according-ly." Several heartbeats passed while his stormy gray gaze collided with hers. "You've told me I'm good at my job. You've expressed confidence in my abilities, intelligence, and judgment. Were you simply saying those things to pacify me, or do you believe them?" His challenge was unmistakable.

Again, long moments went by before Doro found her voice. When she did, it was a low murmur. "Of course, I believe what I said." When Ev again reached for her hand, she did not pull away.

"Then, show it by having faith that I know what I'm getting into," he murmured.

The warmth of his hand was in stark contrast to her icy fingers, but Doro nodded. "All right."

A smile tugged at one corner of his mouth. "Thank you."

Wade cleared his throat. "Ev is right. I'll be hiding close to the bench and watching carefully. Nothing bad will happen. I doubt if the note writer planned to harm Rud, so he won't hurt Ev, either. Besides, we'll create a solid plan."

Although Doro nodded again, she silently acknowledged that plans did not always work out. And she prayed this one would.

゜ﾟ｡

For the next ninety minutes, the group went over the specific strategies for the trap. Doro realized Ev included her and Aggie so she knew exactly what would happen and how. While she appreciated the inclusion, Doro felt no calmer. If anything, her anxiety grew to a suffocating level. By the time the two men prepared to leave, she was almost breathless. Watching Ev strap on a shoulder holster added to the strain.

After Wade did the same, he went to Aggie and the couple spoke softly in the far corner. Doro walked to the front window and stared into the darkness. She felt, more than saw, Ev's approach.

With gentle hands on her shoulders, he turned her to face him. "I'll be fine," he assured her. "Trust me, please."

His solemn expression and intense tone precipitated her response. "I trust you, and I respect your ability as a lawman." Both assertions were true, but they did not mute her apprehension. Despite that, Doro would not burden him with her fears, because they could be distractions, which he did not need. "I know everything will be all right." It had to be.

For several moments, he gazed into her eyes. "This isn't the right time or place for serious talk, but after the brunch tomorrow, let's take that picnic we talked about."

In an effort to be calm and casual, Doro said, "It's a date."

After brushing a featherlight kiss across her lips, he stepped away. Within a moment, Wade stood beside him.

"Let's get going, so we have time for me to find a good hiding place," the constable said.

Ev donned a hat and coat before turning back to Doro. "It'll be an hour or so."

Swallowing over the lump in her throat, Doro could only nod.

After the door closed behind the men, Aggie slipped an arm around Doro's waist. "We should sit down because there'll be a wait."

With reluctance, Doro retook her chair while her friend did the same. A glance at Aggie showed some tension. "You must be worried about Wade."

"I am, but like Ev said, they are experienced lawmen."

"I know." Unfortunately, the knowledge did not lessen her worry.

"But you're fretting, just like I am," Aggie murmured.

When tears pricked her eyes, Doro brushed them away. "I am."

"How about more coffee?"

Doro forced a smile. "My nerves are already jangling, so maybe not."

"Mine, too," Aggie admitted.

Doro searched her mind for a distracting topic. Almost immediately, one came to her. "Did you ever read the letter that Rud handed you the other morning?"

"Curiosity finally got the better of me," Aggie admitted.

"It's getting the better of me, too. What did it say?"

A lilt of laughter left Aggie. "A lot of nonsense about how he wished he'd ignored his mother and courted me years ago, and more foolishness about how he still cared for me. He said we could live in the city, since my poetry is being published. Evidently, he figured we could live on the prize money and royalties."

Doro's jaw dropped. "That cad."

"He had nerve," Aggie replied. "I wonder how long it would've taken before Bonnie moved nearby. You saw him with her. Both of them were smitten."

An image of the pair arose. "It seemed that way."

"Tonight, he asked me for a fast dance. If he'd been enthralled, like his letter claimed, wouldn't he have chosen a fox trot or a waltz?"

Thinking about how she loved being in Ev's arms, Doro concurred. "He would have."

When the jingling of the telephone interrupted, Doro rushed to the counter. "It must be Doc again. I can't imagine who else would call at three-thirty in the morning." After picking up the candlestick base and the earpiece, Doro heard the local operator.

"Another call from Doc," the woman said in a sleepy voice. "I hope there's a good reason for getting me up again."

"There is, but I can't tell you now," Doro said.

A harrumph carried over the line. "All right. Here he is."

"I need to talk with Wade or Ev right away," Silven said.

"They just left for the park, where they're setting a trap for the note writer."

"Can you catch them?" Doc asked. "I've got to get to the Walling place. Their baby is coming, and it's her first."

"Sure, we can do that," Doro replied, although it was not likely she and Aggie could get to the men before they took their places in the park. She planned to try.

"Great. There was another slip of paper inside Rud's sock. I didn't take them off until just now. It looks like the same print, but with more splotches. From what I can make out, it says: ...*be there on time, and don't try anything because I won't be al...* The beginning and end are illegible, but it sounds like more than one guy planned to meet Ingram."

"It does," Doro agreed, nearly breathless with anxiety. "Thanks for letting us know."

"What did Doc say?" Aggie asked as soon as Doro hung up.

Doro stood where she was and supplied a summary. "We have to go after them."

Aggie put her clasped hands to her mouth. "They're probably at the park already."

"Yes," Doro said, "but maybe we can get there in time to give a warning."

Aggie jumped up. "Let's go."

Although her friend was usually circumspect, Aggie was clearly just as worried about Wade as Doro was about Ev. "We can discuss our strategy on the way."

As the two friends hurried through the dark streets, they exchanged ideas about how to proceed when they reached the park. "There are two brick paths leading to the war memorial from the front," Doro said. "There's also a worn dirt path coming from behind it. It's only been there since the brick was laid two years ago. That took time, so people started walking from the main sidewalk back through the woods and up to the memorial."

"I remember. It got worn down pretty fast."

"Mostly kids still use it, but I know it's not overgrown."

"So, we should walk up from there."

"I think so. We'd have a good vantage point to see what's happening," Doro said, before reviewing what she knew. "Ev should be clearly visible on the bench to the west side of the wall, and Wade may take cover on the same side but facing out."

"We'll have a panoramic view from the middle."

"Exactly." As they entered the park, Doro lowered her voice. "We have to be quiet."

"Agreed," Aggie whispered.

For several moments, they crept along, careful not to trip on the uneven ground. When they reached a point where another dirt path branched to the side of the memorial where Ev and Wade planned to be, they stopped. "I didn't know about this lane," Doro murmured.

"Me, either. Maybe I should go that way, since I'd have a better chance of seeing Wade."

Doro chewed on her lower lip. "You can still caw like a crow, right."

"Sure. My brother taught me when I was eight, and I was teaching Wade's son Davey last week."

"Great. If you see Wade, call out."

"Fine, but what if I see someone else? I can warble."

"I can't do either one, but those signs will help. Just be careful."

"Don't worry. I will be."

After Aggie slipped out of sight, Doro moved forward until the memorial came into view. Sitting on one of the benches was Ev, hat pulled low on his head and coat collar turned up. A whoosh of air left her. For now, he was fine, so she scanned the area and did not see anyone. With great care, she crept forward. Was there a way to alert Ev without warning whoever was coming? While she debated calling out, and wished she could make bird calls, Doro kept moving until a hand went over her mouth. For endless seconds, shock froze her in place. Then, she started fighting. She swung her arms and tried to jab her captor with both elbows, but stopped when the barrel of a gun was pressed to her temple.

"Stop it or I'll shoot you."

Doro recognized the soft female voice because it belonged to Cereta Devlin. For a moment, the fight went out of Doro, who was not shocked, only dismayed. Hank had remained a suspect, and his wife would undoubtedly help get their money in any way she could. In the hope of lowering Cereta's guard, Doro remained still. For several moments, the other woman did not react. Then, the hand on the gun relaxed. Doro threw one arm back and caught Hank's wife off-guard. Cereta reeled back and away from Doro. As soon as she could, Doro yelled, "Watch out, Ev."

Cereta swore under her breath and tried to regain control of Doro, but to no avail. Doro flailed around again. When the gun flew a few feet away, Doro ran toward Ev.

By then, he was on his feet and headed in her direction. Even in the lamp light, his alarm was obvious. "What are you doing here?" Alarm etched his face.

Doro had no opportunity to answer because Hank called out.

"Cereta, are you hurt?"

"No, I'm all right, but I lost my gun." The woman's plaintive tone held a world of frustration and regret.

"Get out in the open, Devlin. Your wife, too." Wade's voice came from a copse of birch trees near the memorial.

Several moments of silence prevailed before Hank replied. "Don't hurt Cereta."

"We won't if you both throw your weapons where I can see them," Wade called back.

"Mine is in the deep grass," Cereta yelled.

"That's true," Doro confirmed as she kept moving toward Ev.

"Then, both of you get out here with your hands in the air," Wade said, "and Devlin throw your gun away before you do."

Cereta, hands above her head, emerged first. Within a moment, her husband stepped out from behind a silver maple, threw his gun on the ground, put his arms up, and moved forward.

After a last long look at Doro, Ev asked, "Are you all right?"

"I'm fine," she murmured.

"Good. We'll discuss this later," he said before joining Wade.

Doro wanted to explain but that would have to wait. The two lawmen were handcuffing the Devlins when Aggie joined her.

"What happened?" Aggie asked.

"I'll tell you later," Doro murmured. When Ev shot her a sidelong glance, she did not want to hear what was on his mind. But she had a valid reason for coming, and he better appreciate it.

"I'm eager to hear the entire tale, too," he said.

"As am I," Wade added. "But first, we'll get our prisoners back to the office."

Cereta started making excuses, but Ev shushed her. "You'll get a chance to talk later. Just get going."

Silence fell over the group as they made their way to Main Street. As soon as they stepped inside the constable's office, Wade gestured for the Devlins to sit down by the stove. Then, he and Ev used two more sets of handcuffs to secure them to the chairs.

"Is this necessary?" Hank asked.

"Yeah, it is," Ev shot back. "You brought weapons, and your wife held one on Doro, didn't you, Mrs. Devlin?"

How he knew that, Doro was not sure, but Ev had been in a lot of dangerous situations as a lawman. And Cereta had admitted to being armed.

Tears pooled in Cereta's dark eyes. "I wouldn't have hurt her."

Although Doro was not so sure, she withheld comment. Confirming Ev's suspicion would only increase his annoyance with her.

Ev's implacable expression remained. "Maybe. Maybe not."

Wade perched on the edge of his desk while Ev stood closer to the table. "Let's get down to why you were in the park."

Hank cleared his throat. "Rud had to tell you about the meeting. Otherwise, how would you have known to come to the memorial?"

"So, you were there to meet Ingram," Ev said.

A grimace formed on Hank's face. "Yeah. We were."

"Why?" Wade asked.

Hank's jaw tightened. "He told you why, I'm sure." He glanced around the office. "Where is he?"

The comments reinforced the idea that neither of the Devlins had been with Rud when he fell into the pool. The note worked against them colluding with Rud and Vance, but what was going on?

"That doesn't matter," Wade said. "What we want to know is why did you ask him to bring the book to the park at four in the morning. It'll go better for both of you, if you're honest."

The doctor's shoulders slumped. "Rud took it out of the showcase because he not only owes us money, he owes Vance Smith and some bootleggers. And maybe Adler. He paid part of his debt to the gangsters by rumrunning for them, but he keeps getting in deeper and deeper due to gambling."

"And he keeps saying he can't pay us," Cereta said, her voice shaking.

When he responded, Ev ignored her remark. "How do you know Ingram stole the book?"

Hank's head fell forward. "I couldn't sleep last night, so I took a walk." He looked at Wade. "I haven't slept well for a while due to our financial trouble."

"Everyone knew Wade and I were taking turns guard the book," Ev said. "What made Ingram think he could take it?"

After a deep breath, Rud replied. "After he met Bonnie Adler, Rud walked around town. He's got more problems than I have, so sleep is elusive for him. There was a flurry of activity, so he hunkered down and watched the goings on."

"That must've been when the volunteer firefighters got going," Wade put in.

"Yep," Hank agreed. "It was a lucky happenstance, especially when Rud saw you, Constable."

"Happenstance occurs in real life," Ev said, with a glance at Doro.

"It does," she agreed with a rueful grin.

Ev returned to questioning Hank. "So, Ingram nabbed the book and ran into you afterwards?"

"He did," Hank said. "I agreed not to turn him in, if he paid us. I thought he planned to sell the book on the black market, since he has criminal contacts, but Rud said he'd pay us after getting the reward."

Ev's forehead furrowed. "He knew there would be a monetary reward ahead of time?"

"He told us that," Cereta replied.

Their revelations confirmed many suspicions. "Was Vance Smith involved in the theft?" Doro inquired.

Hank met Doro's gaze. "When I ran into Rud, that's what he said. Vance swore his parents would offer a big reward, and they did. But he didn't help steal the book."

"Did you know Vance was against the reward?" Doro asked.

Hank shook his head. "No, but it could've been a ploy. His parents are rich, and his mother valued the book."

Doro did not disagree.

Ev straightened to his full height. "Why didn't you wait for your share of it?"

A harsh sigh escaped Hank. "When I talked to Rud at the ball game yesterday, he said the money would only cover what Vance and the bootleggers were owed, so we'd have to wait. I was suspicious about our old fraternity getting paid, since Vance talked to the president when we were there between practice and the game. Why should they get some money when we're owed?"

"That wasn't fair," Cereta insisted, her voice bordering on hysterical. "We need those funds for our family."

While Doro understood their panic, she felt less sympathy than she had a day earlier. Having a gun held to her head erased it. "Were you planning to sell the book?"

Cereta's attention moved to Doro. "Of course not. We were going to turn it in and collect the entire reward."

"Your note mentioned turning Ingram in. I suppose you have evidence about him being involved in bootlegging," Ev suggested.

Hank's nostrils flared with a sharp intake of breath. "No solid evidence, just Vance's word but he claimed Rud was afraid of getting caught rumrunning. He didn't want to do it any more, which is why he put paying the gangsters ahead of us. It's why he sold the Stutz Bearcat. He's in deep debt, and working with gangsters is dangerous, you know."

A half-smile tugged at one corner of Ev's mouth. "I do know."

Doro could not help but wink at him. When his smile broadened, she grinned. The Devlins might never discover the depth of Ev's knowledge about bootlegging and rumrunners, but she knew.

"So, you figured the only way to get any funds was to blackmail Ingram," Wade put in.

"Not blackmail," Hank insisted.

The humor left Ev's expression. "Sure sounded like it in the note."

"Is that why he contacted you, too?" Cereta asked. "Was he accusing the note writer of blackmail?"

Ev and Wade exchanged a long glance before the constable responded. "He didn't contact us. We found your note."

"Both of them?" Hank asked in a puzzled tone.

When Ev and Wade looked confused, Doro explained Doc's call without revealing Rud was dead. "That's why Aggie and I went to the park. To warn you that more than one person might be coming."

"I see," Ev said, and his softer expression revealed he did.

"So, how did you find the notes?" Hank asked. "Rud was drinking toward the end of the dance. Did he drop them?"

After a long moment, Ev answered. "They were on his body."

"Body?" Cereta echoed. "What in the world do you mean?"

"Did he pass out from drinking?" her husband inquired.

"We're not sure," Doro replied. "He was found dead at the bottom of the new pool."

Chapter Twelve

Profound silence resonated through the constable's office. Doro watched as the color drained from Cereta's face and Hank's jaw dropped. If they were feigning their reactions, they needed to go into the theater.

"When was that?" Hank asked, his voice thin and thready.

"After one o'clock," Wade told him.

"We were both at the hotel then," Cereta said.

Ev took the chair across from Hank. "We know that, since Wade talked to the proprietor when we got back here."

Cereta's shoulders slumped, and her husband leaned back in his chair. Although Doro had not thought either of them killed Rud, she wondered if they knew who had. Or if they knew the book's location.

"So, are you going to let us go?" Hank asked. "We weren't going to blackmail Rud."

A muscle jumped in Ev's jaw as he ground his teeth. "I could overlook the note, but your wife threatened Doro, and there's no way I'll ignore that."

"I told you I wasn't going to hurt her," Cereta insisted in a plaintive voice. "I wouldn't hurt anyone."

"The barrel of your gun was pressed to my temple," Doro blurted out. Almost immediately, she regretted her impulsiveness because Ev went stark white.

Ev's hands clenched into two tight fists. "Then, she's definitely being charged," he muttered, his voice hoarse and husky.

Tears splashed down Cereta's cheeks. "Please. I have four children and elderly parents. We've been strapped for money because of Rud."

"I overheard the three of you talking in back of the library," Doro admitted, "and you mentioned taking Rud's former patients when Aggie and I ran into you in front of the hotel. Because he moved to the city?"

A crease formed on Hank's otherwise smooth forehead. "Rud gave up the practice shortly after his folks died within months of each other. He never enjoyed living in a small town and didn't make it a secret, so no one was surprised when he decided to move. I'd been seeing some of his patients for a while, since his dad had a long illness. Rud saw fewer and fewer folks himself over the last couple of years."

"I see," Doro murmured, although she really didn't. If Rud's father had been ill, wouldn't he have needed to see more patients? "Why did he move to Toledo?" Although she could guess, Doro wanted to hear the reason from Hank.

"He'd already been going up there whenever he could," Hank observed, glancing from Aggie to Doro. "You two might not have known, but he was in a lot of card games when he was a student."

A frown furrowed Aggie's forehead. "He mentioned playing cards occasionally, but many of the boys did."

A rueful expression crossed Hank's face. "As I recall, he enjoyed it more than most. His last year in school here, he was up until almost dawn on many occasions. But not studying. He struggled to keep up with school work toward the end."

The observation explained why Rud had paid another student to write a paper. "How did he manage to get through medical school?" Doro asked.

"We didn't go to the same place, and I would've been behind him, but I heard from others who were classmates of his that Rud cut back on gambling during his time in medical school. Long enough to graduate, at least." Hank shook his head. "For a while after going home, Rud shouldered his share of the work, but he had a penchant for city life and started heading to Toledo almost every weekend. When his dad was still going strong, he handled most of the practice. As he got weaker, Rud had to pitch in more. Some weekends, Rud asked me to take his house calls, so he could head to the city. I didn't want to ignore sick folks, so I did."

His wife muffled a sob. "That was a big sacrifice, since it meant Hank worked long hours every single day. Rud Ingram didn't care at all. He only cared about himself."

Hank cast a glance at his wife. "You've made the biggest sacrifice, because you had to handle the children and critters alone so much. I'm sorry about that."

When Cereta closed her eyes, tears splashed down her cheeks. "We only wanted to get what he owed us."

"How did the debt get so large?" Doro asked.

"When old Dr. Ingram got sick, he asked me to order the medicines we use for patients. He didn't trust Rud to do it, and we often take drugs on house calls, since folks can't always get to the nearest drug store. Some cures are commonly used, so I kept them on hand and so did the Ingrams. The same with office equipment. I ordered and paid for some that was delivered to the Ingrams' office. Rud was supposed to pay me for everything."

Aggie leaned forward. "From what Rud always told me, the house was fancy. Surely, someone in town could afford to buy it."

"A few could have, and he had two solid offers before the October crash, but he waited for more money. The buyers can't come up with the funds now, so he's stuck for a while at least," Hank replied.

"And so are we," his wife murmured.

While the stock market crash was only starting to affect Michaw, Doro was well aware of economic problems in other areas. "Why didn't he move back and live in the house?"

Hank's jaw tightened as his gaze went to a point beyond the two friends. His overall demeanor was odd, but his response provided some insight. "I don't know it to be a fact, but I believe

Rud has a yen for both liquor and wagering. Those activities are readily available in cities, but not in small towns."

Dead silence followed the observations. A penchant like that both lured people in and held them hostage. Despite living in a small town, Doro was well aware of what occurred in big cities. Her one excursion to a speakeasy, and Ev's revelations, had taught her a great deal.

Aggie shoved her hands in her skirt pockets. "I didn't know Rud as well as I thought."

The flow of conversation provoked more questions. "Did Rud lose a lot of money in the crash?" Doro asked.

Hank's jaw tightened. "He didn't have a large sum to lose at that point. At least, that was one excuse when he didn't pay me what he owed. Rud claimed his folks didn't leave him as much as he figured, but traveling to the city, staying in the best hotels, drinking, and gambling—all that costs money. When he moved, he got a fancy apartment. Nothing but the best for him."

"Rud bragged about all that?" Doro asked.

"He didn't talk much about drinking, just going to speakeasies and getting into special card games for their best customers," Hank replied.

More moisture welled in Cereta's red-rimmed eyes. "While Rud lives the high life, we have to put buckets around when we get a heavy rain. It'll only get worse this summer when more thunderstorms roll in, and I worry about feeding the kids and critters. A garden will help, but it may not be enough, especially now that my parents are living with us. The farm is rented, but at a low rate. I'm not sure how we'll manage without the money from Rud. We adults can wear worn out items, but kids keep growing and need new ones. My mother sews some, but it's hard to keep up with everything. Kids, critters, sewing, gardening, cooking, and all."

Doro's heart went out to Hank and his family. "That's awful."

"It certainly is," Aggie agreed.

Cereta turned a watery gaze on Doro. "I'm sorry I put the gun to your head. I was desperate and not thinking."

"I understand," Doro said, and she did.

His eyes blazing, Ev looked from Doro to the prisoner. "I don't. What if the gun went off?" His voice shook. "Then, you'd be charged with murder."

As Cereta cried harder, Hank tried to reach out to her. "It'll be all right, dear." He sent an imploring look at Ev. "Charge me. I'll take the blame."

Ev, who had taken a chair, rolled his eyes. "That's not how justice works. The person who did the crime is the one who gets arrested."

His harsh tone and frozen expression were so out of character that Doro stared in silence. She was about to ask him to be lenient with Cereta when Hank spoke again.

"Officer Mallow, you're not married, so you may not understand that a husband does whatever is necessary to protect his wife and family. I love Cereta with all my heart and soul, and I can't stand by and see her charged and maybe imprisoned." He turned to Wade. "You and Aggie are engaged, so you must fathom how I feel."

When Ev leaped to his feet, his chair banged to the floor. "No, I'm not married, but I know what it is to love someone deeply and profoundly. I know what it is to be willing to do anything, including die, for that person because that's how I feel about Doro. So, you try to comprehend how I feel knowing your wife held her at gunpoint." The words shot out as fast and furious as bullets from a weapon.

While Ev focused on Hank, Doro riveted on him. As she did, her heart flip-flopped and her eyes filled with tears. Ev had written his sentiments on a Valentine, and he had spoken them, too. But not in front of others, and not so boldly and audaciously. Although she adored him for being so open, Doro did not want to put Cereta Devlin behind bars. Earlier, both Ev and Wade had agreed that justice could take forms other than through the legal system. Would Ev still concur with that?

Hank's blonde lashes fluttered down. "Like you, I'd want the person to pay."

Since Doro figured a discussion of actual charges would be better later, she brought up the primary issue still plaguing them. "Let's talk about that later. What about the book? Do you have any idea of where Rud put it, Hank?"

For a moment, the young doctor stared at her as if he had not understood. Finally, he shook his head, as if to clear it. "Rud refused to say, but Vance knows. Both of them admitted to that yesterday."

"Was their plan to have young Smith return the book ahead of brunch?" Wade asked.

"Yep. He was the go-between with the book and the money," Hank said. "His last plan was to pin it on fraternity pledges. Maybe Vance would've shared the funds with our old house, but I wouldn't count on it. Not when there wasn't enough for Cereta and me. It was likely another empty promise."

"But you don't know where the book is," Aggie suggested.

"No, I truly don't," Hank replied. He shifted restlessly. "Is there any chance of us being put in a cell? That'd be better than this." He jangled his handcuffs.

A long breath left Wade. "If it's all right with Doro, we can lock you up in your hotel room until we get the manuscript back. There's a night desk clerk since the place is full, and I'm sure he'd keep watch, so you don't try to break out."

"We won't," Hank assured the constable, "because that would only make matters worse for us."

"It would," Wade agreed before turning to Doro. "What do you say?"

"That's fine," she replied. Ev's stormy expression indicated he did not agree, but he said nothing. Not that he had since his impassioned speech.

"Ev, will you help me see the Devlins to their hotel?" Wade asked.

A moment's hesitation preceded his agreement and, within a short time, the lawmen and their prisoners left the office. The moment the door shut behind them, Aggie turned to Doro. "I've never heard Ev be so bold."

"Neither have I," Doro admitted.

"Saying he loves you and would die for you. Wow. That was beautiful."

Ev, usually circumspect, never blurted out his feelings or views. Would he regret doing so? His long silence afterwards made her wonder. Doro felt uncomfortable discussing such profound emotions, even with her best friend. "Hasn't Wade said much the same to you? After all, you're engaged."

"He's expressed his love and said he'd do anything to make me happy."

"Which is pretty much the same."

"Pretty much but not exactly, and he hasn't stated his feelings in front of people." Aggie grinned. "Maybe you two will be engaged before summer comes."

Doro's heart strings fluttered like ribbons in the wind, but doubt plagued her. Since the Sweetheart Dance, Ev had not brought up the next step. Would he now? Did she want that?

※

When the lawmen returned an hour later, dawn was already chasing darkness from the sky. Doro figured they would all discuss how to get the book, but Aggie and Wade stepped into the storeroom on the pretense of looking for more coffee and a tin of cookies. Although Doro knew her friend was giving her time alone with Ev, she was not sure they needed it right now. Retrieving the book and figuring out what happened to Rud were of top importance. Besides, she did not want to hear Ev make excuses about what he had exclaimed, and she feared he would.

"Let's sit down." Ev gestured to the table. After she took a seat, he did.

Doro folded her hands in her lap. "You got Hank and Cereta settled."

"We did. I'm not sure I agree with Wade on letting her escape a jail cell, even for a short time but you approved it."

The censure in his tone made Doro straighten her shoulders. "Not long ago, you agreed that justice isn't always served best by using the legal system. Cereta wasn't going to shoot me. I knew that." Actually, she was not one-hundred percent sure but almost.

His jaw tightened and relaxed. "Do you have any idea of how I felt when I saw you running from her? And worse, she'd had a gun to your head." His beautiful silver eyes turned stormy gray as he spoke.

"I'm sure it was upsetting," she murmured. Had he meant what he'd blurted out? That was the foremost question in her mind.

With one hand, he massaged his temple. "Upsetting? That's a weak word. It was devastating. Even with you safe and sound, knowing you'd been held at gun point shattered me." He reached out for her hand. "I didn't make it clear how terrified I was when I found out you and Aggie had been held in a cellar by a killer. But we weren't stepping out then, so it wouldn't have been seemly. And I must not have been obvious about how I felt when I learned you'd been kidnapped from the train." He released a shuddering breath. "We don't have long to talk, but I want you to understand now that you are my world. Whether you ever agree to marry me or not, you'll have my heart and soul forever. If something happened to you..." He swallowed hard. "I couldn't bear it."

One phrase echoed in her head. "Ever agree to marry you? How could I agree when you've never asked me?"

Amazement rounded his eyes. "You know I love you."

"And I love you."

Seconds of silence slipped away before he went down on one knee. A rueful smile moved his lips. "This isn't a romantic place, and maybe you'd like to wait for one."

"No, I don't want to wait," she whispered, her throat tight with emotion and her heart hammering her ribs.

Low laughter rumbled out of him. "Dorothea Rose Banyon, would you do me the honor of becoming my wife?"

She slipped forward to put her arms around his neck. "Yes. Yes, I will." When their lips met in a long kiss, Doro felt his hands caress her back, and she leaned closer. At some point, probably within minutes, Aggie and Wade returned, but Doro was lost in a world shared only with Ev.

"Sorry to interrupt," Aggie said.

Heat rushed into Doro's face as Ev resumed his seat, and she settled back in hers. "Yes, well, that is…that's all right."

Both Aggie and Wade chuckled. "It looked more than all right." He looked at Ev. "You wanted time alone with Doro, and now I know why. Not that I didn't suspect."

Ev, his own cheeks dark with color, lifted his chin. "I said you two would be among the first to know."

"Know what?" Aggie asked, but her grin said she already understood.

"We're engaged," Doro replied.

Aggie threw her arms around her friend, and Wade shook Ev's hand. "I'll make up for the less than perfect proposal place somehow," Ev told Doro.

Wade's eyebrows rose. "What's wrong with the constable's office?"

"Absolutely nothing," Doro said with certainty. Who cared where the proposal took place? Ev had overcome whatever doubts had been plaguing him, and that was far more important.

"I wish we had time to celebrate, but I want to watch Adams' house so we can follow young Smith when he leaves, and I still think he will," Wade said.

"On the way back from the hotel, I told Wade I have a nice view from my room in Maple Hall," Ev added, "so, the two of us will head over there. We're guessing Smith may already have the book, although we don't know how that happened. We'll find out, though."

The idea intrigued Doro. "Should we wait here?"

"We can walk you two to Wheaton Hall. That way you can grab some sleep," Ev said.

Surely, he was kidding because Doro would not doze off with the book still missing and him out searching. "We can wait for you in the reception room."

When Ev did not immediately respond, Wade did. "That's fine."

"Sure," Ev agreed.

The two couples walked through the quiet town without saying much. At one point, Ev let the other pair get ahead of them. "It's not that I don't want you to come along."

"But Aggie and I can't hide out in Maple Hall with you and Wade."

He grinned. "No, you can't."

Doro was about to reply when she saw a male figure walking down the path from near the President's residence. "Ev, look." She pointed to the man.

"That looks like Smith," he murmured before softly calling to Wade who immediately turned around. Ev gestured toward the figure.

Aggie and Wade retraced their steps. "Is that young Smith?" he asked.

"I'm sure it is." Doro kept her voice hushed. "He's coming this way."

Ev clasped her hand. "We're two engaged couples out for an early morning walk."

"We are?" Doro found that an unlikely possibility.

"It's the best I can do on short notice," he whispered, humor lacing his voice.

A smile was her reply. Doro realized the moment that Vance recognized the two couples because his eyes widened and his jaw worked.

Despite his evident surprise, Vance recovered quickly. "Good morning. You're all up early."

"As are you," Doro remarked.

Young Smith grinned at her. "Yep. It's the best part of the day."

"Really?" Doro asked. "When you and your father talked about putting your glad rags on and painting the town red, I didn't figure you to be an early riser."

For a moment, Vance glanced at a point in the distance. When he looked back at Doro, he offered one of his boyish smiles.

"Admittedly, I usually experience sunrise on my way to bed, not getting up from it."

"What brings you out this morning?" Ev asked. "Other than wanting to enjoy the sunrise."

Vance's expression hardened when he addressed the security officer. "Is there some law against me doing that? There wasn't when I was a student here."

"Nope. No law. I just wondered." Ev's simple observations hung heavily in the air.

Wade, a smile on his face, stepped forward. "So, you're just taking a walk?"

"Pretty much." Vance shoved his hands into his jacket pockets. "A bit chilly. I should've worn something heavier."

As young Smith moved, his windbreaker pulled across his chest to reveal a bulge. Doro's attention riveted on a lump, a lump in the shape of a book. Her heart raced with anticipation. While she debated about confronting Vance, Doro took a sidelong glance at Ev whose focus was also on the protuberance. "It is cool," she agreed. "Mrs. Fisher, the head cook in the girls' dormitory, will have plenty of hot beverages at breakfast: coffee, tea, and cocoa. She's serving all the students and any alumni in the boys' residence, due to brunch set-up in the girls' facility. You know where that is." Doro gestured down the route Vance had taken.

"Yeah, sure, I remember reading that in the invitation sent to alumni," Vance said. "I guess I got mixed up thinking it'd be in the girls' dining hall."

"That's empty now since workers won't start preparing for brunch until nine o'clock," Aggie put in.

"I see," Vance murmured. "I suppose it's all locked with no one there."

"It should be," Doro said.

"I might just walk by," he replied. "If you'll excuse me."

When Vance turned away, Ev caught his jacket sleeve. "Not so fast." As he spoke, Ev got between Doro and the other man, while Wade did the same with Aggie.

"Let go of me." As Vance jerked back, his windbreaker opened and a book fell out. The missing book. He rushed to grab it, but Ev was faster.

"How did you get this?" Ev asked, holding the tome up.

Vance's jaw tightened. "You already know I'm the go-between for the person who took it and my folks. I'm charged with returning the manuscript and relaying the reward to the thief."

"I know, but why sneak around?" Ev inquired.

"I'm not sneaking around," Vance insisted before addressing Wade. "Please tell your assistant to return the manuscript to me. I want to get it to my mother."

A pensive expression blanketed Wade's face. "You're not headed toward the President's house. You're going in the opposite direction."

Again, Vance looked at the book in Ev's hands. "Yes, well, I..." His voice trailed off.

"How did you get the book back and who had it?" Doro made her query in a soft, soothing tone. Although the book was no longer missing, they needed to discover what had caused Rud's death. Doc would report his findings, but even a high blood alcohol level would not be conclusive. Someone could have pushed him into the pool and left him to die. Would Vance have done such a thing?

"That's not important," he shot back. "What's important is that it was recovered. I'm the go-between, so I have to return the book so the person who gave it up gets the money."

Ev's nostrils flared with a sharp intake of breath. "We already know who took it. What we need to find out is how and when you got it from him."

"Maybe we should conduct this interview in my office," Wade observed in a cool, flat tone.

A long sigh left Vance. "I'd rather talk elsewhere. Being seen going into or out of the constable's office won't please my parents, if they find out."

"Wheaton Hall is close," Doro said. "We could chat in the reception room. No one will be there so early on a Sunday morning."

"Good idea," Aggie added.

When the lawmen agreed, the group headed to the women's faculty residence. Doro unlocked the door and ushered everyone inside.

After they were all seated on the sofa and loveseats at the far end of the space, Wade addressed Vance. "Tell us where and how you retrieved the book."

"You all know my parents don't want charges filed. That's why I'm involved," Vance insisted.

"We know, but events overnight make it possible that other crimes were committed," Ev said.

Vance's brow wrinkled. "What crimes?"

"Let's go back to who took the manuscript and why," Wade said

"This is a waste of time. I need to pass on the reward money before dawn, and it's getting close." Vance looked from Ev to Wade. "You're the lawmen. Why are you impeding me? You supposedly cared about the book being returned. It has been."

Ev leaned forward. "How and why was it taken and re-turned?"

Vance's blue eyes became slits. "You said you like a job that puts food on the table. If you want to remain as the campus security officer, you better let me go."

The threat hung in the air like a funeral shroud. Doro wanted to chastise Vance, but Ev spoke first.

"You can use your influence if you want, and I might lose my job," Ev said, "but I'm not bowing down to a spoiled playboy."

A guffaw left Vance. "You can always marry Doro and let her support you."

Doro jumped to her feet. "That's enough, Vance. You never used to be such a cad. What's wrong with you? Did you collude to steal the book, knowing your parents would offer a big re-ward? Are you getting a cut?"

"We know who took the book, Mr. Smith," Wade put in. "Being nasty won't change that."

As Vance slumped back, he briefly closed his eyes. "Who do you think took the manuscript?" He direct the query to the constable.

The question did not surprise Doro, since Vance had always been shrewd. "Like Wade said, we know, so there's no sense in dilly-dallying."

His clear blue gaze riveted on her. "How do you know?"

For a moment, Doro debated about revealing the truth. Then, Ev winked and she went ahead. "Hank Devlin told us. He was taking a walk early this morning and ran into the thief."

"That, I didn't know," Vance muttered. "But Rud was cagey."

When the admission slipped out, Doro grinned. "He needed to be, considering his debt level."

"And the number of folks he owed," Wade added.

A long exhalation left Vance as he faced the lawmen. "Yeah, he got into money trouble a few years ago. For a while, he siphoned funds from the practice, but his father got on to it. Rud had to borrow then."

"Due to gambling," Ev suggested.

"Yep. He couldn't quit, and debt piled up and up. At first, I felt sorry for him," Vance replied. "Then, I got fed up with never getting paid back, so I quit making loans to him."

"Is that when he started rumrunning?" Doro asked.

Surprise lit Vance's gaze. "Hank told you?"

"He did," she agreed.

"You don't want to owe money to gangsters, so Rud had little choice. Mostly, he helped bring booze across Lake Erie from Canada, but making enough runs to finance his wagering proved difficult," Vance observed.

"So, he ran up more debt with gangsters," Ev said, "and didn't pay others he owed when he sold the Stutz Bearcat."

"That's right," Vance said.

As she considered what else the Devlins had revealed, Doro formed her next comments. "Hank and Cereta need what Rud owes them, but he didn't plan to pay off that debt, did he?"

Vance shifted restlessly on the loveseat. "What makes you think that? My folks offered a hefty reward."

"It is generous," Doro agreed, "but would it cover what you are owed, along with Rud's debt to gangsters, and to the Devlins?"

Vance's gaze narrowed on Doro. "I've heard about your amateur sleuthing, and you've always been sharp, so I'm guessing you know a whole lot more than you've admitted to draw me out."

Doro could not repress a grin. "We may have some additional details." A glance at Ev revealed he was fighting a smile, so she returned her attention to Vance. "You'd be wise to tell us everything. You already stated not wanting to go to the constable's office. As things stand now, you aren't in the clear in a couple of ways."

Confusion clouded Vance's blue gaze. "I'm not sure what you mean."

"You haven't revealed how you got the manuscript from Ingram," Ev said. "Doing that might help your case."

Or clinch his guilt in Rud's death. Doro waited to see which way things went.

Vance threw both hands into the air in a gesture of surrender. "All right. I met Rud last night right after the dance. The deal was that I'd put the manuscript on the head table in the girls' dining hall ahead of the brunch and let my parents think the culprits sent me a note that they felt remorse for taking it. I'd be the go-between to hand out the reward, but the thieves would remain anonymous."

"Culprits? Thieves?" Wade asked. "Were you planning to pin it on pledges?"

"I talked to the president of my old house, and he was willing to let people think his pledges were involved as long as I made a nice donation," Vance replied. "Some of them were out last night, as it was. Mostly, doing odd jobs for the brothers."

The memory of seeing her student rose in Doro's mind. Evidently, Brian had told the truth, so

She focused on the main issue. "When and where did you and Rud meet?"

"Around midnight in the park near the war memorial," Vance replied. "He was drunk, but he brought the book."

"Did you argue?" Wade inquired.

Vance shook his head. "No. Why would you think that?"

When Wade did not answer, Ev jumped in. "What happened after you got the book?"

"I left," Vance said in a clipped tone.

"What about Ingram? What did he do?" Doro posed the questions.

"He said Bonnie Adler was coming," Vance revealed. "The two of them met Friday night, too. She was smitten with him when we were students, and they ran into one another at a speakeasy a few months ago. After she moved out of her sister's house and into an apartment with some other girls, Bonnie saw Rud pretty often. I think he's sweet on her, too, but he's a poor candidate for marriage."

"That's for sure," Aggie blurted out before clapping a hand over her mouth.

A frown darkened Vance's features. "It's not like you to be so judgmental, Ag. Or has engagement to a copper changed you so much?"

"That's none of your business," Wade said.

Since Vance had already made important admissions, most of which cleared him in the killing, Doro got down to brass tacks. "Rud is dead."

Vance's jaw dropped. "What? When? How?"

His utter confusion seemed genuine, but Doro let the men continue the disclosures.

"His body was found last night in the park," Ev said.

"In the pool," Wade added.

"By Bonnie?" Vance asked.

Ev leaned forward. "No, Doro and I were walking our dog near the pool. Ingram's body was at the bottom."

Silence reverberated through the expansive space before Vance braced his elbows on his knees and put his head in his hands. "I can't believe it. He was still drinking when we met after the dance, and I said he should lay off, but he kept at it."

"He had a flask?" Wade asked.

"Yeah," Vance said. "He always carried one."

"We need to go back and look for it," Wade said to Ev.

"Maybe Bonnie has it," Vance offered. "She was meeting him, and she liked a nip herself."

Although Vance seemed to be shocked by Rud's death, he could be acting innocent and pinning the blame elsewhere. "We only have your word that Rud was alive when you left the park."

"I didn't kill him," Vance blurted out. "There was no reason for me to do that. None at all."

"Maybe, maybe not," Ev said.

"What about Bonnie? Did you talk to her?" Vance inquired. "Rud had promised to pay her father some money, even though the old man is confused about the deal. But there wasn't enough for that. He wasn't going to take her back to Toledo with him, either. He couldn't without more dough. She might've pushed Rud into that pool."

"Before we delve into that, where were you going with the book?" Ev lifted the rare tome into the air.

Vance sighed. "Like I said, my old fraternity will take the blame Since no charges will be filed, the president is willing to meet me at the girls' dining hall. We can easily get in those French doors and leave it on the head table."

Ev and Wade exchaged a long look. "I want to speak with Bonnie Adler. Will you escort Mr. Smith to his meeting."

"I sure will," Wade said.

After getting to her feet, Doro addressed Ev. "I'd like to go with you."

He grinned. "I hoped you'd say that." Ev handed the manuscript to Aggie. "I'll leave this in your hands."

"We'll keep it safe and secure in Wade's office," Aggie replied.

Chapter Thirteen

On the way to the Adler house, Ev took Doro's hand. "Bonnie may be more open with you, but let's start by asking if she heard people again last night instead of saying we know she was meeting Ingram."

"That's a solid plan. If she wonders why we're at her door just after dawn, are we still looking for the manuscript?"

"Yep. We'll wait to reveal we know Ingram is dead. You're good at gauging how and when to provide bits-and-pieces, so I'll leave the timing up to you."

His confidence in her buoyed Doro's spirits. "I'll do my best."

Ev paused mid-step and turned to face her. "You always do, which is only part of why I love you so much."

Her heart hammering in a staccato rhythm, Doro rose to her toes and pressed a kiss to his lips. For a moment, he stood stock-still. Then, his arms went around her, and he returned the kiss.

Long moments passed before, breathless, Doro pulled away. "Even engaged couples need to be circumspect."

His silver gaze glittered. "Engaged. It's a beautiful word." He took her hand again, and they moved on.

When they reached the Adlers' front door, Doro pointed to the small window. "There's a light coming from the kitchen."

"Stu is used to getting up early, so he may be fixing breakfast." Ev rapped on the wood.

In a few moments, a figure appeared in the hallway. "It's Bonnie," Doro said. The girl opened the door only a crack, so seeing her face was impossible. "Good morning. I'm sorry to disturb you so early again, but we had a couple of questions."

"I have to fix breakfast before Pa and I go to church," Bonnie replied.

Since the entire town worshipped at the community chapel, and those services did not commence until ten o'clock, Doro pressed for cooperation. "You have lots of time, and we won't keep you for long."

After an interlude, Bonnie opened the door and turned toward the front parlor. "We can talk in here."

Because the drapes remained drawn and no lamps were on, the room was dim. Bonnie gestured for Doro and Ev to take the love seat while she sat in the rocker some twelve feet away. Making out her features proved impossible. "You know we've been searching for the manuscript," Doro said.

"Yes. You told me yesterday morning," the girl replied in a hoarse voice.

"Are you sick?" Doro asked. "You sound congested."

"I'm all right," Bonnie murmured.

"I hope you are," Ev said. "If you don't mind, I'd like to jot down some notes." With one hand, he pulled a pad out of his jacket pocket while, with the other, he pulled the chain on the lamp beside him.

When light flooded the room, Bonnie put her hands to her face but not fast enough to conceal her red and swollen eyes. Doro's heart clenched. Had the girl caused Rud to fall into the pool? Accidentally? Intentionally? She hoped not, but she needed to know. "What happened last night when you went to meet Rud Ingram?"

A stricken expression drew Bonnie's pretty features into a tragic mask before tears fell. Seconds passed while she sobbed quietly. "He left the dance early. Pa and I weren't there much longer, so I should've been able to meet him right after midnight. I was fifteen minutes late because Ma didn't feel well, and she wanted me to sit with her. Rud and I were meeting at the bench closest to the new pool, but he wasn't there, so I looked around." Her voice grew almost inaudible before she swallowed hard and went on. "I finally went to the pool area and saw a flask on the ground. When I started to pick it up, I caught sight of something..." Sobs overtook her.

Doro glanced at Ev who motioned for her to continue talking. "You realized it was Rud."

"Yes," she croaked. "I called to him, but he didn't move. I kept calling and calling."

"Did you know he was dead?" Doro asked.

"I wasn't sure," Bonnie replied. "I feared he was, but I hoped he wasn't. I hoped he'd wake up and climb out after he got sober."

"Did you know he was drunk?" Ev inquired.

A shrug lifted one of her slender shoulders. "He drank almost every night, usually too much. Since the flask was empty, and he'd consumed alcohol during the party, I figured he had to be."

"And you left him there." Doro was confounded by that idea.

Bonnie's lips trembled. "I couldn't be found with him. Not in the middle of the night. My pa would've been plenty mad. He didn't even like Rud and me talking."

"Your reputation matters more than your feelings for him." If Ev was laying hurt or wounded, Doro would not walk away from him. But she wasn't smitten. She was deeply in love.

"I don't want to stay in Michaw, but my folks need me here," Bonnie shot back. "They wouldn't have thrown me out, but I would've been shunned. People might've stopped coming to the bakery, since there's one in Sylvania. We couldn't afford for that to happen."

"If Rud had asked you to marry him, would you have left?" Doro posed the question in a clipped tone, because she knew the answer.

"Yes, but we would've been able to help my folks with the money from the reward," Bonnie insisted.

"You knew about the plan to take the book and about the reward," Ev said.

Bonnie clasped her hands in her lap. "Rud told me after he stole it, so I'd know we could get married after he got the money. That was what he said at the dance tonight."

"Where is the flask?" Doro asked.

A shaky breath left Bonnie. "I brought it with me, because I wanted something of his. It's engraved with his monogram."

Tears again flowed down her face, and she wiped them away with the back of a hand.

"We need it," Ev told her as he flipped the notepad closed. "We may also need you to come to the constable's office later this morning."

"What will I tell my folks?" Bonnie asked.

Although Doro felt sorry for the girl, she made a direct reply. "You should have thought about that a while back."

❊

When Doro and Ev got to the constable's office, Vance Smith and the fraternity president were leaving. They brushed past the pair without a word.

"I see you've still got the book," Doro said as she and Ev sat down at the table with Aggie and Wade.

"I called President Adams. Ev and I can take it over after the Smiths are up," Wade said. "I'll let him handle the fraternity and his boy."

"How did their son escape without Adams seeing him?" Ev asked.

Wade frowned. "Young Smith was able to slip out a window to meet Ingram around midnight, and he did the same thing this morning. He hurried back and was just coming downstairs when Doro called. I don't know what story he'll tell his parents, but Adams is still against charges being filed, so I reluctantly agreed."

"What about Cereta and Hank?" Doro asked.

"We could get him on attempted blackmail, but I'm not inclined to do that," Wade replied. "As for Cereta, that's up to you, Doro. She held you at gunpoint, which is serious."

As Ev sat forward, tension laced his lean body. "It sure is."

Doro laid her hand on his forearm. "I don't want to press charges. Cereta was desperate to help her family, and I don't think she intended to hurt me."

For several moments, Ev studied Doro. Finally, he nodded. "Probably not."

"Then, I can let them both go," Wade said.

Ev nodded. "If that Doro wants."

"Thank you," she murmured.

"Let's leave them locked in their room until after we deliver the book," Ev said. "They shouldn't get off the hook too quickly."

"Fine with me," Wade agreed.

Doro did not disagree. "Are you going to bring Bonnie in?"

Ev turned to Wade. "The girl is devastated, so I'm sure she told us the truth."

"I agree," the constable said. "We'll need an official statement from her, but it can wait until tomorrow." He looked at his fiancé. "Why don't you and Doro get some rest? You've got a few hours before the brunch."

"What about the two of you?" Doro asked. "Will you take a break?"

"Later," Ev promised. "For now, we've got to get the book to Adams and talk with the Devlins before releasing them."

"I want to talk with Doc, too, if he's back from delivering the baby, which is iffy," Wade added. "As things stand now, maybe we should meet you girls at the brunch."

"That's best," Ev agreed. "We'll have to clean up before then."

"All right," Doro said, although she wished the men had a chance to relax. "We'll see you about quarter to one."

A grin lightened Ev's weary expression. "I'll look forward to it and to our picnic later."

Although she had been anticipating their private time together, Doro offered an out. "Maybe you'd like to rest after the brunch, since you have to be exhausted. We can have a picnic next weekend."

Ev shook his head. "I'll never be too tired to spend time with you, but I might doze off."

A sudden image of his head in her lap, his dark lashes resting against his skin, sent yearning through Doro. As an engaged couple, they could partake of innocent, informal actions. "I wouldn't mind," she murmured. "I wouldn't mind at all."

Chapter Fourteen

While Ev and Wade took the book to the Smiths, Doro and Aggie returned to Wheaton Hall for some welcome rest. Following a long nap, Doro dressed and went to her friend's apartment, where she found Aggie ready to go.

As the pair walked to the dining hall, they exchanged greetings with others, so private conversation was impossible. Doro could not repress a smile when she caught sight of Ev who, with his hair still damp and his face clean-shaven, looked as handsome as ever. Not even his obvious exhaustion detracted from his appeal.

The group exchanged greetings before Wade suggested they move aside for a private talk. Once they were some thirty feet from the dining hall entrance, he spoke again. "The Devlins headed for home after we let them out of their locked room. Ev and I made it clear that Mrs. Devlin could still be charged, so they need to patiently wait for their money."

"After the Ingram house sells?" Doro asked.

"Yep," Ev replied. "It's a bit of a penalty. She deserves more, but I know how it is to care for a family with limited means."

"I'm sure they appreciate the leniency," Doro observed.

"I hope so," Ev said.

"What happened when you returned the book?" Aggie asked.

Her fiancé turned to her. "President Adams and the senior Smiths couldn't thank us enough. Their son wasn't present, but his mother said he regrets being involved. The father insisted he only wanted to help an errant fraternity brother."

"Errant? That's a mild term for what Rud got himself into," Doro said.

"For sure," Ev added. "The book will be presented as planned, and young Smith will be at the head table. His folks are willing to donate funds to his old fraternity, mostly because the father had been a member, too, but the reward is null and void. Adams has some clean-up around campus for the fraternity."

"Good," Aggie said. "I don't think anyone deserves the money under the circumstances."

"I concur with that," Doro put in. "What about the blood alcohol test? Was Doc able to determine Rud's level?"

"Luckily, Doc has experience doing those tests from his intern days. He wasn't home, but his wife shared the results," Wade said. "Ingram's was high enough that Doc believes he could easily have been stumbling around."

"The comments from Vance Smith and Bonnie Adler support the findings, so we can wrap up both cases with reports," Ev said.

Their conversation ended when Mrs. Jones and Floyd Quartine approached the quartet. After both commented on the latest developments, and expressed their sorrow over Rud Ingram's death, the entire group headed inside.

Brunch proceeded with no additional complications, but Doro yearned for it to end, so she and Ev could escape for some private time. Bidding farewell to the guests wrapped up her responsibilities, but Mrs. Smith called her aside after the dining hall emptied.

"Vance told us you were instrumental in finding the book. I cannot tell you how much that means to me. I know it's in good hands with you."

"Thank you, ma'am. We'll treat it like the treasure it is," Doro assured her.

"I also wanted to let you know that when Mr. Quartine retires, as he plans to do soon, I believe, I'll support you being the next director. I've told President Adams as much. Michaw College has always been progressive, and having a woman in an important role will keep the school on that path."

Doro smiled. "I'm grateful for your support, but would you feel the same way if you knew I'd be the director and a married woman?"

A grin took years off the older woman's face. "Absolutely, my dear."

When Ev joined them, he said, "I don't want to interrupt."

"Is this the lucky man?" Mrs. Smith asked Doro.

His twinkling gaze landed on Doro before looking at the other lady. "I'm her fiancé, if that's what you mean."

"It is," Mrs. Smith said. "Congratulations and best wishes to both of you. Now, I should get going. Vance is anxious to get back to the city." She shook her head. "He says he wants to be in the office with his father on a daily basis. I don't know what caused his sudden change of heart, but I hope it lasts."

After she walked away, Doro rolled her eyes. "Nearly being arrested might be the reason."

"I'm sure he's relieved," Ev said, "and Cereta Devlin is, too. Thanks to you."

His grim expression made Doro lay a hand on his arm. "We've already agreed she wanted to help her family. Despite the gun, I don't think she would've hurt me."

"Probably not," he agreed. "And they'll have to wait until the Ingram house is sold to get their money, which is a little punishment."

"Punishment is such a strong word."

"I'm a lawman, remember?" His gaze searched hers. "I hope you won't regret marrying someone beneath you."

She lightly smacked his arm. "You are not beneath me, Everett Mallow, and never say so again."

A grin lightened his expression. "Yes, ma'am."

"What are you agreeing to?" Wade asked after he and Aggie joined Doro and Ev.

"Anything and everything my girl wants," Ev replied.

"Is that a promise?" Doro asked with a wide grin.

He clasped her hand. "It is, and it's only one. I want to make other ones in the near future."

"Me, too," Doro murmured, and she knew exactly what vow they would make.

"As long as we are discussing making promises, Wade and I have something to tell you," Aggie confided. "We've set a date. July 11."

Doro hugged her friend while Ev slapped Wade on the back. "Announce the wedding publicly soon, because I can't wait long to have everyone know Doro's agreed to be my wife. I don't want to steal your thunder, but..." His voice trailed off as he focused on his fiancé. "You're not thinking of a long engagement, are you?"

She shook her head. "There's a two-week break in January between semesters. We could even squeeze in a honeymoon trip."

"Sounds perfect to me," he murmured.

"Me, too," Doro whispered back. "Absolutely perfect."

Thank you!

Thank you for reading <u>The Doomed Doctor.</u> I hope you enjoyed it. For more about Doro's sleuthing adventures, please visit my website, where you can sign up for my newsletter, if you have not already done so. News about future releases, promotions, other authors', historical tidbits, and more are in the monthly missives. https://dslangbooks.com

If you want to know more about what led up to this story, there are five books in my Doro Banyon Cozy Historical Mystery series. Each is a standalone whodunit, and the first, <u>The Catalogued Corpse</u> is free. You can find links to various digital retailers at https://dslangbooks.com/series/All of the ebooks are also available through my online store, the Bijou'd Boutique. You get 20% off your first order with coupon code FIRSTORDER.

Doro Banyon Cozy Historical Mystery series

The Doro Banyon series has a cozier tone than the Arabella Stewart books. History and mystery still mesh as amateur sleuth Doro solves whodunits with a team of colorful characters in smalltown America during the 1920s. Travel back in time to a college campus and crack cases with them!

Prequel-<u>The Lost Exam</u> (free when you sign up for my newsletter)

Book 1-<u>The Catalogued Corpse</u>

Book 2-<u>The Murdered Matron</u>

Book 3-<u>The Jammed Judges</u>

Book 4-<u>The Problem Professor</u>

Book 5-The Bottled Bootlegger

Book 6-The Doomed Doctor

Book 7-coming November 2025

A Valentine's Day short story, "The Vintage Valentine," is available to my newsletter subscribers. In it, college librarian and amateur sleuth Doro takes a break from detective work as she prepares for a romantic evening at the annual Sweetheart Ball with her would-be beau, Everett Mallow. Will this be the night when they go from stepping out to courting? Or will a snowstorm interfere? A vintage Valentine plays a role in this standalone story, which is not a mystery but has a thread of suspense.

You can sign up for my newsletter at https://dslangbooks.com

Arabella Stewart Historical Mystery series

The Arabella Stewart Historical Mystery series is set in small-town Ohio after the Great War. Bella returns home from serving as a U.S. Army Signal Corps operator to find her family resort and hometown in dire straits, and the murder of a neighbor adds to the trouble. Much to the dismay of Constable Jax Hastings, an Army veteran, Bella turns amateur sleuth to solve the case. As the series continues, Bella and Jax vanquish the shadows of the war, while solving a series of whodunits with a team of colorful characters. Love and laughter occur along the way. If you love history and mystery mixed with touches of humor, romance, and drama, this series is for you!

Book One-A Precarious Homecoming

Book Two-A Lingering Shadow

Book Three-A Lethal Arrogance

Book Four-A Baffling Absence

Book Five-A Fatal Reunion

Book Six-A Surreptitious Undertaking

Book Seven-A Treacherous Accusation

Book Eight-An Uncertain Ceremony

Two prequels for this series are available to my newsletter subscribers. Sign up on my website: https://dslangbooks.com You can unsubscribe at any time!

About the Author

D.S. Lang, a retired educator, started making up stories to entertain herself as an only child, and she is still making them up. Now, she puts them in writing. She is an avid storyteller and reader, with a To Be Read stack that is overflowing. In her free time, D.S. enjoys swimming, reading (of course), spending time with family and friends, and walking with her dog, Izzy.

A lover of language, D.S. has published over 10 books, with more on tap. Her aim is to write novels that blend history and mystery with dashes of drama, splashes of humor, and touches of romance to create charming stories with authentic details. When you finish one of her books, she hopes you have a smile on your face!

Set during the post-Great War period in small-town Ohio, the books welcome readers into an exciting period of American history, when women were navigating new roles, and the country was dealing with Prohibition and the aftermath of war. Living through those times required spunk, which her amateur sleuths have in spades.